BEACH SHORTS

Edited by

Susan Tulio, River Eno and LCW Allingham

Dedication

To Rob, Frank and Tom
and endless summer days on warm sandy
beaches

Contents

For years I spent summers at the Jersey shore, and I distinctly remember the used bookshop located a short block away. For me, it was a treasure chest disguised as a run-down, musty smelling beach cottage with buckled floors. The inside overflowed with gemstone-colored books in every genre. The back room was where I spent most of my time. Floor to ceiling shelves held every historical romance I could have wished for: covers plastered with a half-naked Fabio and voluptuous beauties dressed in corsets and billowing skirts.

With *Beach Shorts* I wanted to create that same feeling of walking into that cool Jersey bookstore. Countless stories at your fingertips with a selection to choose from that you could read in order or jump around.

Beach Shorts holds a bounty of surprises. The stories that came across my desk were charming and packed with romance, a little bit of magic and a lot of fun.

Tidepool Dreams, Shark Out of Water and *Mermaid and Coyote* are three stories filled with love, laughter and promises made by the water's edge. *Tea Leaves* follows a woman's quest to fulfill a fortune told. In *True Romantics* and *Blueberry Bells,* we witness a great love and a reunion of two souls.

A romantic attraction is just the beginning for two members of a bridal party in *The Best Man.* Sparks fly between a jogger on a collision course with an artist in *Muffins and Meet-Cutes,* a clever set up becomes too tempting to resist in *Lemon Drops at Mermaid Lagoon,* and a life built on lies finds truth and a sweet reward in *Tangled Web.*

In *Wildwood,* a well-deserved second chance at love takes us back to a simpler day. Falling further into the past we follow a rivalry that turns romantic in *A Race to Finish.* *Ultimate Timeshare* takes us even deeper back in time with an escape to Sparta.

I love an anthology that is easy to read and filled with the unexpected. *Beach Shorts* is a collection of romantic short stories that are the perfect length when you are limited on time. When life interrupts, you'll be able to pick it up again and jump back in.

I remember leaving that bookstore and wanting nothing more than to crack that romance novel open the second my toes hit the sand. However, with three small children, a stolen moment was all I could ever manage. I'd end up reading a chapter and then have to put it aside. An anthology like *Beach Shorts* would have been a better choice. Each story would have offered the freedom I needed, the romance I craved and the happy ending I hoped for.

Whether it's a sizzling love story, a romp in the waves, or a melancholy reunion of two hearts, I can't wait for you to find all that and more within the pages. I am so excited to offer this collection and hope when you come across the table of contents that you feel like a kid on the lookout for treasure.

-Susan Tulio

Tidepool Dreams

C.N. WHEATON

"My grandma is a pelican."

Most people would have given me a look at an announcement like that, but Alan wasn't just anyone. I met him for the first time that summer on California's central coast, although it felt like I'd known him all along, as if our friendship had always existed and was just waiting for us to catch up. Alan smiled at me, listening.

In retrospect, maybe I should have wondered why he didn't have any problem with the idea that my grandmother was a pelican, but crushes can make a person overlook a lot.

"She always liked the idea of reincarnation. She also loved to eat. When I asked her why she wanted to be a pelican, you know what she said? 'Look at how much food they can fit in their bills!'" I laughed. Then I looked out over the ocean, grief like a riptide pulling me under. My next words came out as a whisper. "She's been gone for two years, but every time I see a pelican it feels a bit like getting a hug."

Alan slung his arm around my shoulders. I nestled into him, breathing in his scent of salt and sunshine. All too soon he let go. "That's why you love coming to the beach, isn't it?"

"Yeah," I agreed. "But spending time with you is pretty good too." That was an understatement. Alan made ordinary moments magical.

Maybe I should have wondered about that too.

"Callie, thanks for telling me about your grandma," he said, his normally teasing tone serious. "She sounds really special."

I smiled, remembering. Being there with Alan made me think of all the good parts, all the laughter and love. Alan and I stayed there on the sand until the sunset was fading from the sky. The sand was cold beneath our toes as we left the beach. He walked me back to my family's little rented bungalow, and I found myself wishing the summer would never end, that this could be our always, that he could be my forever.

The next morning Alan arrived right as I was finishing up breakfast. My little brother spotted him first and ran to let him in. As Alan entered, he waved jauntily at my mom, and she rolled her eyes, smiling. She loved him too, my beachy, beautiful boy. "I'll have her back before dark," he promised.

"You kids have fun," Dad said from his spot on the couch, not even looking up from his book. He'd happily stay like that the whole day. I kissed his head as I went by, and he absently patted my cheek before turning to the next page.

"Take sunscreen. And a hat," Mom said. She'd always been the more practical of the two. There were no pelicans in her family tree.

"Where are we going?" I asked when we got out to the porch. Thanks to my mom, I was carrying a little backpack stuffed with sunscreen, water bottles and sandwiches to share.

"It's a surprise!" Alan insisted, flashing that quicksilver grin of his.

I couldn't help but smile back. We walked a long way, the opposite direction from where we usually spent the days running around in the surf, stretched out on the sand, or trying all the sweets in town. I followed him to a little pathway in the bluff above where the sand gave way to rocks. He spread his arms wide as proud as if he'd invented the ocean.

I wrinkled my nose, looking at the dark rocks. They were kind of pretty in a rugged sort of way, but didn't seem like they were worth the long walk. "*This* was the big surprise?"

Alan shook his head at me. "When have I steered you wrong?"

"Last week, when you insisted a second ice cream cone was a good idea," I reminded him.

He winced at the memory. "Yeah, that wasn't the best afternoon, but I'm sure you're going to like this. We've come this far. Just give it a chance?"

I looked dubiously at the narrow path down to the rocks. "Okay, but you have to go first."

"Don't worry, I won't let you fall," Alan said in a teasing tone. He took my hand, and I stopped being afraid. I'd have followed him anywhere, I realized suddenly. I loved him in that fierce, wide-open way it's easy to do when you're young.

When we got down to the bottom of the path, he helped me pick my way out over the slippery rocks, parts of them covered in algae and seagrass. At one point, when he lifted me down from a particularly large rock, I forgot how to breathe for a second. I wanted him to kiss me, but I didn't know how to ask.

Then he led me to where he wanted to go, and I realized why we were there. "Tidepools?" I asked. The last time I'd been tidepooling, I'd been very little and it had been my grandma who'd been holding my hand to keep me safe.

Alan's eyes lit up. "Surprise! I've wanted to bring you here for a while, but the tides haven't been right. Now is the perfect time for it."

My friends from school might have laughed to see how excited I was, but I didn't care. The school year felt a world away. We picked our way across rocks next to a field of shiny black mussels, closed tight as they waited for the water to return.

Then we reached the nearest tidepool.

The rocks that looked so forbidding from far away were hiding their own little worlds. It was more colorful than I'd expected. When I took a closer look, I could see that algae covered the rocks in shades of greens, browns, reds and yellows. On the rocks farther out, their hard edges were obscured by long strands of seagrass that looked black or green depending on the light. The water was cold and clear, shining like a mirror, inviting us to go through the looking glass into the world down below.

Spiny purple sea urchins had always seemed more like pincushions than living things, but he showed me how to gently touch them and wait for their spines to close around my finger as if they were saying hello. A sea anemone waved tentacles of neon green. When I touched one of its brownish-yellow cousins, it felt almost sticky from the sting my skin was too thick to feel. Whether disappointed or scared, the anemones closed up at our touch, going from flower back to bud again, their soft parts covered in shattered bits of shells. Alan pointed out a prehistoric-looking chiton, flat and armored, with eight shimmering segments. Once he showed one to me, I was able to find more amongst the rocks, although none were as beautiful as the first.

He reached into the water and handed me a bright blue shell, threaded with brown. I looked between Alan and the shell curiously. "Wait," he urged.

I stared at the shell, almost dropping it in surprise when the hermit crab unfolded its legs from inside and started to walk across my hand. What had looked like little rocks at the bottom turned out to be dozens and dozens of hermit crabs, jostling for space or position before retreating back into their temporary homes. "Go on home, little buddy," I said as I set the crab, now closed up, gently back into the tidepool. We stayed there, watching it walk away.

We explored, looking for the sea stars he swore smelled like garlic. Even though we didn't find the slimy, mucus-covered leather stars, we found other sea stars hiding in the crevices of the rocks. "You know they eat by pushing their stomachs out, right?" he shared, pretending to demonstrate with his arms.

"Gross," I scoffed even though I actually thought it was pretty cool. He grinned.

In one tidepool we even found a large purple-brown slug he called a sea hare. We watched it slowly make its way across the bottom as we ate the sandwiches my mom had made for us. "You know, I'm happy you're here," Alan shared, his quiet confession the only sound other than the waves.

"I am too," I said, leaning my head against his shoulder. He smiled at me and brushed a crumb away from the corner of my mouth. Alan leaned forward, a question in his eyes. I closed the rest of the distance. The kiss was gentle and sweet and a little bit clumsy. It was better than I'd imagined; it was real. I could have died right then and there, I was so happy.

But, if I had, I'd have never learned his secret.

We walked back slowly. I was smiling so much my cheeks started to ache. He'd held my hand on the way back up the cliff path and had just kept holding it as if it was the most natural thing in the world. The sun started to set, painting the sky in pink and gold, but Alan was good as his word, and we were back in town well before dark.

My family's beach rental was in sight when I asked, "Why don't you ever let me walk you home?"

He stopped walking for a second. When he spoke his voice was strained. "It's hard to explain. I'd have to show you."

"Okay," I replied, confused. "So, show me."

Alan leaned forward and kissed my forehead. "Not tonight," he said as he drew back. "But soon, I promise."

I wondered about his promise as I lay in bed that night, but I couldn't make heads or tails of it. Finally, I decided it didn't matter. I might not know everything about Alan, but I knew that every moment I spent with him was more special than the ones without him. When I slept I dreamed of the tidepools.

We didn't talk about it again for days. I'd almost forgotten about it, too caught up in the heady experience of having someone to kiss, but Alan remembered.

He took me back to the tidepools the next week, pointing out a washed up piece of bull kelp as we picked our way across a small stretch of sand, although it was obvious he was distracted. "What's wrong?" I asked.

"I want to tell you a story," he answered, but his tone was too serious for the words he was saying. When he saw I was listening, he continued. "There was once a seal who was also a woman. She had a magic coat that became her second skin. She could take it off to walk along the shore, learning all the stories of the tidepools, or she could put it on and swim through the waves deeper than any human could ever go. She loved that she could be both. But a man who saw her change stole her coat to keep her for himself. It took her years to find it again, to get back to the ocean she loved. But by that point she had a son."

"I don't understand," I said when it was clear that he had finished.

"Don't you?" Alan asked with a sad smile. He walked over to some rocks and rummaged around beneath them until he pulled out a dappled gray cloak. "My father shouldn't have taken my mother's coat. Things would have been different if he'd asked, or she'd offered." There was something pleading in his eyes. I crossed over to him, cupping his cheek with my hand, standing on tiptoe to kiss him, the coat between us.

"Do you want me to ask?" My voice was soft. This was impossible, but it felt true.

He shook his head. "I'm offering. I have to leave to go back to the water. Unless I don't. If you take this, I can stay with you."

I accepted the coat, hiding it under my bed back at the rental. Alan and I spent every minute we could together. But I knew the summer wouldn't last forever.

Not long before my family had to leave, I asked to walk out to the tidepools again. We laughed and joked all the way, holding hands. The sea shimmered in the sunlight. He didn't ask why my backpack was heavy. I think he knew.

After exploring for a few hours and kissing whenever we found something new, the tide started to come in. I almost chickened out before I saw a pelican soar overhead, the sign I didn't know I needed. I set my backpack on the rock and pulled out Alan's coat. "I love you," I confessed as I pressed it into his hands, "but I don't want you to give up anything for me."

He leaned forward and kissed me. "I love you too. Will I see you next summer?"

I nodded, trying not to cry. With one final kiss I could feel all the way to my toes, Alan stepped back to the edge of the rocks and swirled the cloak over his shoulders. Between one blink and the next, Alan was gone and a seal was on the rocks in front of me. I blew the seal a kiss before he disappeared into the water.

"My grandma is a pelican and my boyfriend is a seal," I whispered to the waves, smiling at the absurdity of it all. Then I turned and walked home, already dreaming about next summer.

Tea Leaves

NATALIE ZELLAT DYEN

I thought I'd have to drink the tea, but Madame Julia took care of it. Good thing because I hated tea and thought fortune-tellers were phonies. But Marilyn, one of my roommates, had insisted we all have our tea leaves read. So there I was at Madame Julia's Psychic Readings on the Atlantic City Boardwalk, two doors down from Steel's Fudge. Marilyn and Bonnie had already had their readings and were waiting for me outside. Afterward we would compare notes over a seafood dinner.

The three of us had rented a bungalow in nearby Ventnor for two weeks, a final post-graduation fling before we headed off to different cities to start our new jobs and grown-up lives. We had agreed that each of us would be responsible for planning an evening's entertainment, and the others were obliged to go along. Tomorrow, at Bonnie's suggestion, we'd be spending the night at The Dunes, a noisy bar with a house band, where they packed you in like sardines, making verbal communication challenging and physical communication pretty much mandatory. Thank you, Bonnie! When she said it was a great place to meet guys, I reminded her that crowded bars weren't my style because I wasn't a flirting-one-night-stand kind of girl. She reminded me that I'd be free to plan something more my style when it was my turn, and I'd already decided it was going to be a barbecue. We'd invite all our friends down from Philly. What better way to celebrate the end of summer?

Madame Julia wore a silky multicolored dress that fluttered and flowed when she moved. With her dark curly hair that was partially tamed by jewel-encrusted barrettes, and her heavy makeup, she looked like a Gypsy character straight out of central casting. The batik-curtained room had that ubiquitous hippie shop smell. As I watched Madame Julia do her thing, I wondered who had decided patchouli would be the smell of peace, love and crystals.

Madame Julia's bangle bracelets jingled as she flipped the cup over onto a saucer and told me to think about my question—the same question the three of us had decided to ask: "Who am I going to marry?" Though it was 1968 and the women's movement was all about liberation and independence from men, I'd bet anything that most single women would have secretly asked that same question. From what I could tell, romance was never out of date, and marriage still figured into the equation for those of us who liked men.

Madame Julia's bangles went heavy metal as she rotated

the cup three times. Then she had me place my hands over the cup and concentrate on my question. Yes, I'd ask the marriage question, but I had my career to think about, so marriage could wait. Judging from my track record, I suspected marriage might not be in my future for a long time. My relationships so far had been half-baked: When the sex was good, the other stuff wasn't and vice versa. Would I ever get to taste the three-layer cake with the buttercream frosting?

Madame righted the cup and rotated it, studying the leaves from all angles. She was frowning—not a good sign. The room was silent, save for the sound of the bangles and the tinkling of the tiny bells hanging from her pendant earrings. The spicy, earthy patchouli smell hung heavy in the air, and I found myself being seduced by the mystical vibe. Maybe there were "more things in heaven and earth…" Was it possible this woman could actually see my future?

My skepticism returned when she pointed to the patterns inside the cup and, in a low, mysterious voice told me what she saw in the leaves:

"The leaves reveal good fortune. I see a journey in your future. There will be challenges, but you will find success in your chosen profession. You will have many friends. You will live a long life…" And so forth.

Such wisdom I could have gotten from a fortune cookie.

Then her expression changed, as did her voice, suddenly strong and decisive.

"There will be a celebration. There will be men in your life, but I see an artist in your future." She pointed to a line of tea leaves. "Yes," she said. "An artist. Wait for him. Hold out for the artist."

When I left the shop, I spotted Marilyn and Bonnie leaning against the boardwalk railing, chattering away. Marilyn had already attracted the attention of at least two men who pretended they were looking at the ocean. How could she not stop traffic? At five foot nine, slim yet curvy, with an olive complexion and straight dark hair, shiny as silk, she had an irresistibly exotic look. More south sea island than South Philly. Marilyn would be moving to LA next month to fulfill her dream of becoming an actress. She'd already starred in two TV ads—a commercial for toothpaste featuring her perfect white teeth, and one for shampoo showing off her perfect black hair—and would be appearing in a cigarette commercial before she took off for the west coast.

One of the men had turned his attention to Bonnie. No surprise there. Bonnie was a sparkling Tinkerbell of a woman (if Tinkerbell had a tiny waist and big boobs). Barely north of five feet, she had a pixie haircut, a wide smile, and she bubbled with enthusiasm whenever she talked. Bonnie had gotten a job with the Philadelphia School System and would be teaching second grade in the fall. The kids were going to love her.

Then there was me. I had two things going for me. A man would have to get close to notice my most notable feature— eyes the color of aquamarine, framed by long, lush eyelashes. The second was my sense of humor—a little too sharp for some, but a source of amusement for many. The rest of me was average; brown hair, freckles and a little pudgy, which unfortunately was not a desirable body type in the Twiggy age. If I were writing myself as a character, I'd make myself beautiful because female protagonists were never unattractive. One of the many reasons I had chosen writing as my career.

Marilyn spotted me, and I waved and joined them.

"So how'd it go, Katie?" they asked me simultaneously.

"You two go first," I said, "then me."

Marilyn flashed her trademark toothpaste smile. "She said I'm going to make it big in the movies even though I didn't ask that question, so she must be the real deal. And I'd have a life of adventure and would eventually marry someone rich, famous, possibly of royal blood. She thinks his name begins with L."

"I'm going to start out teaching elementary school," said Bonnie, "but she predicted I'd find my true passion before I turned thirty, and I'd go down a different professional path. She couldn't see what that path was, but she said that's when I'd meet my husband. We're dying to know what she told you, Katie."

"Honestly, I don't believe a word of it," I said, lowering my voice in imitation of Madame Julia. 'You will have a long and happy life. You will find success. You will find fortune, and blah blah.'"

"What else?" asked Bonnie. "Who are you going to marry?"

"She said there was an artist in my future." I pointed to a

round-faced guy in a beret sketching caricatures two for five dollars. "Yeah, probably someone like that. Just my luck."

"Well, I see oysters in our future," said Marilyn. "Just our luck, Abe's Oyster House is only a block away."

The next morning, the three of us were sitting around the breakfast room table, window open, drinking coffee and enjoying the salty breeze, reminding us we were only a block from the ocean. I'd just volunteered to put breakfast together when the sound of slamming car doors and loud male voices drowned out our conversation.

"That's annoying as hell," said Marilyn. "I'll tell them to keep it down." She went to the window, looked out and signaled the two of us to join her. We watched as three guys unloaded a station wagon parked in front of the house next door.

"Let's get our suitcases inside and grab some grub," said a tall guy in a faded Harvard sweatshirt.

"All we got is beer," said his friend, who was shirtless and tanned to burnished copper perfection. "We'll have to do some shopping."

"Check out those abs," whispered Bonnie. "I call dibs."

"Beer for breakfast!" said Harvard.

"So uncivilized, Len," said the third guy. He was facing away from us, so all we could see was his sandy blond ponytail and the back of a well-worn madras shirt. "Don't you know it's uncouth to start drinking before ten."

Marilyn cocked her head and whispered, "Harvard is mine. He's super cute, super tall, and his name starts with L."

"If Harvard is yours, and Mr. Coppertone is Bonnie's," I said, "that leaves me with Ponytail Guy." I was hoping to see his face, but he'd already gone inside. My friends had won the lottery, but I'd have to wait for the winning number.

"I'm going to get this party started," said Marilyn, and was out the door and chatting with Harvard and Mr. Coppertone before I could finish a sentence. She pointed to our window, they waved, and we waved back. When the guys had gone into their house, Marilyn yelled up, "They're coming over for breakfast. Set three more places."

I volunteered to make pancakes, much more manly than the yogurt and granola we'd planned.

"Howdy, neighbors," said Marilyn when Len and Mr. Coppertone arrived. "Y'all make yourselves at home." She'd subconsciously taken on the speech patterns and mannerisms of the character she'd be playing in the cigarette commercial. Though the cowboy's girlfriend only had one line, she was determined to make it memorable.

"That's right neighborly, of you," Len mimicked in a friendly way, handing her the beer.

Bonnie took charge of the seating arrangements: the two guys on one side of the table, my two friends at either end, and me across from the men, next to an empty chair.

"Pancakes okay with you guys?" said Marilyn.

"I'll speak for all of us in saying yes to pancakes. I'm Len, by the way."

Mr. Coppertone scowled. "Len thinks he's entitled to speak for all of us since he just graduated from Harvard and thinks he's hot shit. I'm Alan, and just a lowly Franklin and Marshall grad. Our friend Danny is on his way."

Marilyn had pushed her chair back from the table, crossed her impossibly long legs, which looked even longer in tight-fitting capri pants and angled her chair toward Len. "How long'll you guys be in Ventnor?"

"Two weeks," he said, his eyes on her legs before redirecting them to her face.

"Same as us. Cool. What'll you be doing this fall?"

As the two of them continued their conversation, Bonnie angled her chair toward Alan. "And what about you, Alan?" She put her hand on his upper arm. Bonnie was a "toucher." Not in a suggestive way, but rather as an extension of her bubbly persona. Alan didn't seem to mind at all.

I observed their body language, the easy flirting, the natural pairing of people who were obviously attracted to each other.

"Well," I said to no one in particular, "breakfast isn't going to make itself."

The small galley kitchen was just off the breakfast room. As I mixed the batter, I looked out the little window that faced the back of our bungalow and the one next door. No sign of Danny. With that ponytail, I thought, he *could* be an artist. That would be one hell of a coincidence, something that might happen in a cheap romance novel but not in real life.

And anyway, why was I even thinking about artists?

I flipped the pancakes, picked up a bottle of maple syrup and set it down in the center of the breakfast room table. No Danny. No big deal. If he didn't show up, I'd just serve the pancakes and head to the beach where I could finish a story I was working on.

I cooked two more batches and piled them on a serving plate.

"I come bearing pancakes," I said as I brought the last of the pancakes into the breakfast room. The late arrival was standing behind his two buddies. Danny. He smiled. I froze. He had a dimple on one cheek. My stomach fluttered. Chiseled features, full lips, pale blue eyes. My heart raced. "Coup de foudre" the French called it. Thunder bolt. Lightning strike. I'd always thought love at first sight was something that existed only on the pages of Harlequin novels or in musical theater, like "You may see a stranger across a crowded room." Leave it to me to see a stranger across a stack of pancakes. I giggled.

"What's so funny?" he said, his voice light as an Irish tenor, "I think you better put those pancakes down or you'll be wearing them. Sit down, I'll grab the seat next to you, and you can tell me what you're thinking."

"What I'm thinking?" I said, putting the platter on the table and sitting down next to him. "Wouldn't you like to know."

"Actually, I would."

But how could I tell him my insides had turned to Jell-o

when he smiled and showed that dimple? So I steadied my voice and told him about my dreams of being a writer.

"I've been hired by Random House as an administrative assistant. I'll be moving to Manhattan in September."

"Random House," he said. "Impressive."

"Not so much. I'll probably be fetching coffee and buying anniversary presents for my boss's wife."

"It's a start. I get the feeling you'll be moving up. You seem like a…scrappy gal."

I laughed. "Scrappy? Like Nancy Drew?"

"Nancy who?"

"It's a girl thing. And what about you?"

"Electrical engineering. Graduate school at Columbia."

"Maybe we'll run into each other in the big city?"

"I think I'd like that."

Hold out for the artist.

Shut up, Madame Julia. There's something special about this guy, and I'm sticking with him.

We had so much to talk about: growing up in Philly, and the difference between word people and number people, and his younger brother who was a pain, and my younger sister who was a pain. On and on until there was a lull in the conversation, and we were surrounded by silence.

"I didn't realize everyone left."

"Me neither," he said. "I think I was too distracted by your eyes. They're incredible. Never saw eyes that color."

I think every inch of my body was blushing then, including parts that had never blushed before.

We continued our conversation on the beach under his umbrella. Our friends were stretched out nearby on beach towels, tanning. Marilyn was lying on her stomach. She'd unfastened the top of her two-piece, and I watched Len rub oil on her back. He was smiling. Maybe later I'd ask Danny to smear lotion on my back. I'd never unfasten my top…not on the beach…at least not yet.

We took dips in the ocean, rode the waves, dried off in the sun, then dragged our blankets back under the umbrella because I told him I burned easily. His legs were so much longer than mine. He had to be six feet. The blond hair on his legs and chest stood out against his reddish tan. If I turned over, would he stare at my butt? Not a good idea. I closed my eyes and drifted off.

Madame Julia: I told you to hold out for the artist.

Me: He is an artist. He probably draws pictures of circuits and wires and such, which would make him an artist, right, so leave me alone.

My stomach growled. "Well that's embarrassing."

"Not really. It's after three, and we haven't eaten since breakfast. Maybe we could grab a bite. You know the area. Suggestions?"

We went to Sack O' Subs a couple blocks away.

"My parents used to take us to the White House Sub Shop in Atlantic City," I said. "It was famous, and we all loved it except my little sister. She'd sit there with her arms crossed, complaining that the lunch meats were gross, and why couldn't we get hot dogs. Such a fussbudget. Did your family eat out?"

"Sometimes, but my brother could never find anything he liked. Such a pain. One time he—"

The waiter came by with our order, and I dug into my sub since I hadn't eaten a bite at breakfast. Danny finished before I did, and sat quietly as I worked on my sandwich, head down, trying to chew with my mouth closed.

"How long have you been writing?" he asked, leaning forward. I held up a finger and washed down the last of my sub with a gulp of soda.

"I don't remember a time when I wasn't writing. Maybe in utero, but only because I didn't have a pen."

He laughed. "What do you write about?"

"A little bit of everything. Relationships, fantasy. I have an idea for a novel and I'm just starting..."

"Excuse me," he said. "Sorry to interrupt, but there's a piece of something next to your lip. No. Other side. You're not getting it. May I?" He wiped it with his finger and my cheek tingled. Did he feel it too? Does electricity actually pass between two people who are attracted to each other. Too soon to ask the electrical engineer, but I hoped our relationship would progress to the point where the two of us shared more electrical exchanges.

We walked on the boardwalk. Unlike the Atlantic City boardwalk, which was commercial, the Ventnor boardwalk was residential. We passed women pushing baby strollers, kids running zigzag and clowning around, families dragging their beach chairs and umbrellas off the beach. We were so lost in conversation, I didn't realize how late it was until the lamplights went on.

"Danny, would you like me to show you the beach where my family spent our summers?"

"Absolutely."

We walked a half mile or so to the Ventnor pier, then down the ramp to the beach, sharing childhood memories. Then we stood hand in hand, each lost in our own thoughts. A waxing moon hung bright as a Christmas ornament over the ocean, and I wondered if I was about to take a bite of that elusive, mouth-watering three-layer cake.

How do you know you've found love?

Maybe it's when you're sitting on the rocks at the very tip of the island, and he tells you his father died in a fire when he was fifteen, and there are tears in his eyes. And you tell him your mom got sick and began wasting away until there was hardly anything left of her, and he holds you and brushes away your tears.

Or perhaps it's when you rent bikes at six a.m. and ride all the way to the end of Atlantic City, and you pass an arcade, and he says he thinks you need a teddy bear, and he's going to win one for you. And that night you carry a teddy bear the size of Rhode Island back to Ventnor.

Or it could be when he gives you a tennis lesson and nibbles your neck when he stands behind you, correcting your backhand, and you drop the racket and turn around and kiss him long and hard and say, "We don't need no stinking tennis," and he agrees with his whole body.

"Hey, do you and Danny want to join the four of us for music and drinks at Bayshores?" said Bonnie. The six of us had spent some time together on the beach the past week and shared a few dinners, but we'd mostly gone our separate ways.

"No thanks, I think we're up for a quiet night at home."

"His place or yours?"

I shrugged.

"Well," she said with a wink "I hope it's not *too* quiet."

My evening with Danny began with just the right level of quiet as we sat on the front porch glider, watching the fireflies put on a light show and making out like horny teenagers.

"Did you know those flashes are the firefly language of love?" I said when we came up for air. "Looks like there's a whole lot of loving going on." We had waited long enough for the inevitable, and I was going to make the first move, take the first step as a liberated woman of the sixties who knew what she wanted.

"Let's go inside," I said, my voice husky.

"Yes," he said, letting me lead him by the hand into the bedroom I shared with Marilyn. He took a step toward the bed, but I whispered "no" and leaned against the closed door. "Here." I took off my tank top.

"Here," I repeated. "Now."

I closed my eyes, my nipples hard, anticipating the warmth of his mouth on my breast. Waiting for his tongue to…

"I can't," he said. I opened my eyes. "I can't," he repeated.

"Don't worry, I'm on the pill." I tried to pull him close, but he drew back.

"It's not that. I can't because I'm seeing somebody."

"This is a joke, right?"

"No, Katie. I'm so *so* sorry, but it's not a joke. I thought…"

"You thought *what*?" I crossed my arms over my breasts. "You thought this was a game? Like I was a toy to play with until you went back to…whoever the hell she is."

"It's not like that. I feel something for you. I felt myself falling in love with you. But I'm still in love with her."

"Well, isn't that nice for you." I picked up my tank top and put it on. The clingy fabric covered my exposed flesh but not the raw, damaged rest of me.

"I should have…told you…said something…didn't mean to hurt you…make it up to you…" He put his hand on my shoulder, and I slapped his face. *I actually slapped his face!* "Don't touch me! Just go. Get the fuck out of my face." I tried to open the door, but it was locked. *Fuck.* I fumbled with the key, *fuck-fuck,* but finally succeeded in turning it. "Out of my life!"

"Katie…"

"OUT!"

And he was gone, leaving me with a broken heart and a giant brown teddy bear with a painted-on smile, mocking me from the dresser.

"Wipe that smirk off your face." I grabbed a knife from the kitchen and plunged it into its chest, where the heart would have been if it had one. I slashed at that teddy bear until half the stuffing was on the floor. "That's what you did to me," I said, ripping out the rest of the stuffing and leaving a shapeless mass of fake fur on the floor.

I didn't have it in me to clean up the mess, so I ripped a sheet of paper from my notebook, picked up a tube of Marilyn's crimson lipstick, and scrawled "Sorry, I need this room tonight," and taped it to the door. Let them think what they wanted. I'd explain in the morning.

I grabbed Marilyn's nightgown and a clean set of underwear and took them to the other bedroom, which had a bed and a futon. I thought I should probably move Marilyn's makeup kit to the other room. "But let's be honest, Marilyn," I said aloud, "you don't need no stinkin' makeup." My hysterical laughter quickly morphed into sobs, and I collapsed onto a pile of moldy-smelling teddy bear innards. Catching sight of myself in the floor-to-ceiling mirror— flaming red eyes, chunks of cotton sticking to my tear-drenched face like a drunken Santa Claus—I knew I had to do something to stop my maudlin trajectory into Harlequin hell.

I stood in front of the mirror and brushed off the white stuff that insisted on clinging to me. As I wiped my eyes, I was reminded of an Eleanor Roosevelt quote about inferiority, which I paraphrased: "No one can break your heart without your consent. And you, Danny, do *not* have my consent, so get your grubby hands off my heart."

Tacked to the wall was a to-do list for the barbecue I'd planned for tomorrow evening. Last thing I wanted to do was be the gracious hostess, but we'd already invited the guests and bought the food, so I had to make it work.

Next morning, after I told my friends what had transpired the night before, they offered to take over supervision of the barbecue. Said they'd understand if I bowed out of the party. I was tempted, but I realized that spending the night alone nursing my wounded self was the worst thing I could do. So I told them the preparations would keep me occupied during the day, and I'd put on my big girl panties and soldier on.

As I put the last of the hot dogs and hamburgers I'd bought into the fridge, I practiced the lines I'd say when I ran into Danny at the party. And I molded my face into the cool facade I'd display as I delivered my lines. When Bonnie told me Danny had gone back to Philly, I gave her the "that's nice but no biggie" look, though inside I virtually cried with relief. Now I could get through the evening without constantly looking over my shoulder and girding myself for confrontation.

The party was called for four o'clock, and I went inside a

half hour earlier to get dressed. The grill, tables, chairs, etc., were in place, and our friends from Philly were starting to roll in. I'd hoped for a beach barbecue, but Ventnor didn't allow them after six p.m., so we had to settle for the empty lot behind our house. Along with our friends, we'd invited the neighbors, figuring they wouldn't complain about the noise if they were participants.

The sound of guitars and singing drifted through the open bedroom window. Someone yelled, "You can play anything as long as it's not Kumbaya."

I might have felt like shit, but I was determined not to look like it. I pulled a long gauzy peasant skirt out of the closet along with a flowy turquoise blouse that matched my eyes, which thankfully were no longer red. I applied dark mascara to accent the color of my best feature and treated my lips to crimson lipstick and lip gloss. Putting on my longest, dangliest earrings, I turned to face myself in the full-length mirror, afraid I'd look like a hooker, but surprised myself by looking damned good. A bit exotic, a bit Madame Julia-ish, but younger and without the bangles.

You saw a celebration in my future, Madame Julia, so you can thank me for making your prediction come true.

Grill burger. Flip. Toast rolls. Check hotdogs. Repeat.

Grill duty was a way of being at the party and not being there at the same time. A little small talk, a little eye contact, not too much.

Grill. Flip. Toast. Check. A few more beers and I'd be ready to join the party—something I had to do. It wasn't healthy to play the victim role regardless of how I felt. *He* was the one who deserved to feel ashamed. Probably did since he wasn't here. If someone invented a schmuckometer, he'd be off the charts. I chuckled.

"It's good to see you smile."

His voice. I looked up. "What the hell are you doing here?"

"Huh? All I said was it was good—"

"I *know* what you said. And I asked what you were doing here."

"What do you mean?" He looked puzzled, which made him a better actor than Marilyn.

"After last night."

His eyes widened. "All I wanted was a burger. Medium rare."

"Damn it, Danny," I said, loud enough to turn heads.

He laughed, said something I couldn't hear and laughed again. Buddy, you just broke the schmuckometer. Enough! I raised the spatula, primed to smack him in the face as I'd done last night, but this time with a weapon.

He grabbed my wrist and gently took the spatula from my hand, setting it on the table.

"I should have known," he said. "He loves to ignore my existence. Trust me, I'm not Danny. I'm Josh."

"Don't lie to me. You look...Oh my God. *You're* the younger brother."

"By three minutes."

I opened my mouth but nothing came out.

"Let's start over," he said. "Hi, I'm Josh." He extended his hand. "And you are...?"

"Katie," I managed to croak, taking his hand.

"Pleased to meet you, Katie."

Danny's double. Same face, same everything, down to the madras shirt. He smiled Danny's smile. Identical twins, identical genes. Identical tendency to be a jerk? I abruptly pulled my hand from his. I wanted to turn and flee, but his eyes on mine fixed me in place.

"I have a confession to make," he said. "I lied about the burger. I really came over to give you this." He handed me a piece of paper. "I've been watching you from over there." He pointed to a beach chair a few feet away. "Sorry, that sounds creepy. I swear I'm not a pervert. It was just something about the way you moved, the shimmery dress, the smoke from the grill. And now, close up, I see your eyes are...I've never seen eyes like yours. Damn, I keep sounding like a letch."

I looked at the paper in my hand. A black and white sketch. Of me.

Madame Julia: I told you to hold out for the artist.

Me: Don't pat yourself on the back just yet. He might be a crappy artist.

Madame Julia: Did I tell you what kind of artist to hold out for?

"Did you just say something?" said Josh.

I shook my head and focused on the drawing. It looked

like me, but also made me look like...I don't know...some kind of goddess. Is that what he saw?

"I don't know what to say."

"Say you'll let me draw you again. This time in color, so I can do justice to those eyes."

I was frozen somewhere between "this is bullshit" and "what the hell's happening here?"

"I can see I'm making you uncomfortable."

"Yes...no...I don't know."

"Tell you what. Why don't you find someone to take your place at the grill, and we can go somewhere and talk? Let me show you I'm a nice guy." He smiled a Danny smile. "How about the beach?"

Uh-oh. That's where I went with Danny that first night. Was I setting myself up for a rerun? Even though this one was an artist, I'd have to be extra vigilant for signs of potential heartbreak. "Okay, but let's make it the boardwalk."

We chose a bench under a cone of light from a nearby lamppost, maintaining a respectable distance between us.

"Let me guess what happened with Danny," he said. "He was coming on strong, and just when things were...really heating up...he bailed. Said he was in love with someone else. May have said he was falling in love with you."

Once again, my mouth dropped open, which he took for confirmation and continued.

"Dollars to doughnuts he wasn't lying about falling in love with you, even though he was probably serious about someone else. Danny's done this before. He doesn't mean to hurt anyone, it's just that he has trust issues, probably because he was dumped by a woman he was about to propose to. I told him he should talk to a shrink or someone about why he keeps repeating that pattern."

"Sounds like you're the younger but wiser brother."

"That's me." He looked out at the ocean. It was a clear night, and the moon was almost full, casting a mirror image of itself on the surprisingly calm Atlantic.

"Listen, can I ask you a favor? Feel free to say no," he said.

"Depends on what you ask."

"Could you walk over there, out of the artificial light?"

"And do what?"

"Stand against the railing. The moonlight is perfect." He picked up his notebook.

Madame Julia: Do it!

Me: I can't go through that again.

Madame Julia: You won't. The leaves don't lie. Do it! Enjoy the moment.

As I walked toward the railing, my pendant earrings jingled.

Okay, Madam Julia. Here goes.

I twirled, bathed in the magical moonlight. A passing couple smiled, and I smiled back and twirled again.

"I love it," said Josh, laughing, notebook in hand. "But you'll have to stop twirling, so I can sketch you."

He posed me, and I stood like a statue for I don't know how long, thinking of all that could go wrong, and then all that could go right. This time I'd be careful with my heart, and I had a feeling he would, too.

He said he wanted to do more work on the sketch, so he wasn't going to show it to me just yet. Outside my door, we gave each other meaningful looks. When he kissed me on the cheek, I silently thanked the gods of romance for forcing me to take it slow. I'd undressed his brother in my mind the day we met, and look where it had gotten me.

"Hey, maybe we can go up to the A.C. boardwalk tomorrow," he said. "I'd like to try some of those saltwater taffies. And I hear Steel's Fudge is the best."

"Yes, let's do that."

And maybe have your tea leaves read.

True Romantics

ADRIENNE CLARKE

Whenever someone asked for the story of how she met her husband, Lana was tempted to give them a fairy tale: *Once upon a time there was a boy and girl who loved each other very much*...because so many seasons of her life with Ben did resemble a fairy tale, but in the end the truth was just as romantic. It all began with a poem. Wordsworth's *Composed Upon Westminster Bridge* to be exact. She was at university, taking a course on the romantics, when she heard Ben recite the words:

> *Earth had not anything to show more fair*
> *Dull would he be of soul who could pass by a sight so touching in its majesty*

Lena was enthralled. She loved the way his hair rose from his forehead in a swirling widow's peak before falling in a dark cascade to the nape of his neck. And when Ben told the professor, in his deep, resonant voice, that poetry had changed the way he saw the world, Lena knew she had to be near him for the rest of her life.

On their wedding night, they went to the Lake District, visiting Wordsworth's old home at Dove Cottage and retracing the poet's favourite walks. When they came to the edge of Grizdale Forest, they stopped for an open-air picnic where they toasted each other with Elderberry wine, a romantic favourite. Once the sweet liquid touched his lips, Ben said, "Make me two promises."

Lena leaned her body towards his until their foreheads were touching. "Of course."

"Promise me that we'll always be true romantics, even when we're old and grey. That we'll never forget the importance of truth and beauty in even the smallest things."

The gravity of Ben's expression made her smile. He resembled his romantic heroes in so many ways. Playful, grave and passionate all at once. "I promise," she said, her voice more solemn than when she'd recited her vows earlier in the day. "What's the second promise?"

"That we'll never give up on our dreams–no matter how impossible they seem."

She laughed. "You want us to live on love?"

Ben pulled her in for a kiss. "Always."

"I can promise both of those things, but I want one from you as well."

Ben put one hand over his heart. "Anything."

"Promise me that we'll never be separated. Not ever."

And they remained true to their promises. Like true romantics they camped under the stars; went for walks in the woods; read Keats to one another by candlelight and presented each other with handwritten love poems. On the weekends, they sat in light-filled cafes laughing over lattes and browsing old bookstores for Bronte novels. Together, they created a world of two that made their friends jealous and contemptuous in equal measure. Still, their life wasn't immune to hardship and disappointment. Some dreams, fragile as butterfly wings, aren't meant for the harsh realities of the modern world.

Ben's poetry, adored by Lena, met with so many rejection letters they made a collage of the offending papers. At first, they laughed, marveling at their whimsical creation of paper and editorial blindness. But once the collage grew so large it covered their bedroom wall, Lena noticed that Ben averted his gaze every time he entered the room. One day, she came home to find the collage had been replaced with azure blue paint. "So, we can always have clear skies," Ben told her, his voice a deeper shade of blue than the walls.

"I love it," she said, throwing her arms around his chest that smelled like summer rain.

He held her close, and she could hear his heart beating. "A true romantic would cherish the existence of an ordinary man," he whispered. "No grandeur and glory here. Just me. Do you mind very much?"

"You're all the grandeur and glory I need," she said, her heart beating in time with his.

Ben repeated almost the same words to her when after months of trying to expand their world of two, the sight of blood in her underwear brought her to tears. Lena wondered if it was greedy to want more happiness when she'd already received so much, but still the ache lingered.

And so, continued their life as true romantics, with fewer lines of whispered poetry but no less love or passion. They still held hands on their walks in the woods and sat beside one another in dimly lit restaurants with medieval paintings on the walls. At night, they lay on their bed, intertwined, and watched the stars painted on their ceiling shimmer in the darkness. Together, they watched dreams rise up and out of their bodies like ghosts but leave their souls intact. Their souls endured it all.

Ben kept his poet's heart, but eventually became a teacher where he hoped to inspire a love of poetry in a generation of kids who preferred memes and Minecraft over nature and nuance. Many of his efforts were met with hostility, and worse, indifference, but every now and then a student would write an impassioned verse on true beauty and Ben's face would light up like the morning star. A true romantic could find beauty anywhere. Even inside the grey, weary walls of a high school classroom where occasionally a blade of new grass would grow up between the rows of desks.

Lena's longing for a child couldn't be cured by poetry or solitary walks in the woods. Like her favourite romantic, Mary Shelley, she dreamed dark dreams of blood and monsters when yet another baby was taken from her too soon. After each loss, Ben held her tightly, whispering words of comfort in her ear. If it hadn't been for his arms around her, she felt as though she would have lost all gravity and floated away on the wind like one of Wordsworth's daisies. Without Ben, she would have withdrawn into a place so deep and dark the sun would never find her again. But Ben was there, and they sat together under the old oak tree in the backyard reading Kubla Khan and dreaming of the exotic, faraway places they would visit one day.

One day. Their one days stretched out in front of them filled with hopes and dreams and plans for the future they knew was theirs. Like true romantics, they held the promises they made to one another so tightly they were imprinted on their skin. They would visit the Keats-Shelley Memorial House in Rome and retrace Byron's impassioned steps in Greece. They believed in the power of fate, never doubting that she was on their side. A powerful, yet benevolent force, they blessed her for the twists and turns that brought two kindred spirits together.

Their separation happened so quickly Lena couldn't believe it was real. She knew Ben so well, every curve and hollow of his body as familiar as her own. She could summon his presence just by closing her eyes: the scent of his skin; the feel of his soft black curls, gently threaded with grey against her fingertips, and the sound of his voice, warm and sweet in her ear. He was there beside her just like always, and then, within the space of a breath he was gone.

Lena stared at the policeman who came to her door uncomprehending. He didn't belong in her world with his close-cropped hair, uniform the color of a dark bruise, and most of all the obscene bulge at his hip that concealed a weapon. She frowned at him and shook her head, willing him to disappear. She didn't want to hear his voice, hard and brittle, with no music in it. But the policeman stayed long enough to tell her that Ben was gone. "A car accident," he said, the words reverberating in the air, ugly, discordant sounds. She felt the air rush out of her body, leaving her gasping on her doorstep, clutching the scratchy, blue cloth of the policeman's uniform as if it were the only solid thing left in the world.

Lena learned there was no poetry in sadness. No beauty in suffering. Unrequited love was no bright star, but a dark and endless night from which she could not wake. Ben's abandonment left a gaping wound that bled and bled until she was too weak to stand. Time stopped. She made it stop by refusing to speak or eat or leave the house. So long as she did none of these things, she wouldn't feel her life go on without Ben. The elderberry wine turned sour in the bottle, and she drank every drop; the memory of its former sweetness eclipsed by the bitterness coursing through her wasted body.

Her world of two no longer intact, well-meaning friends and family invaded the dark forest of her grief. They poured endless cups of weak tea and pressed her to eat the morsels of toast they placed in front of her. Desperate for them to go away, she ate and drank and forced herself to smile. After the last hanger-on left, Lena began to breathe again. She remembered Ben's books of poetry and retreated to their bedroom to read them. She read until the words danced in front of her eyes, and her body mercifully gave way to the oblivion of sleep.

Like a true romantic she dreamed strange dreams of love and loss and falling stars in a midnight sky. She dreamed of Ben who constantly reached out his hand, but every time Lena tried to take it, he disappeared. She awoke each morning, her body frail like an old woman's yet filled with longing. During one of his nightly visits, however, Ben finally spoke. *I wrote you a poem. Did you find it?* Lena shook her head and Ben leaned forward and whispered in her ear.

She found Ben's poem pressed inside the pages of Keats' collected letters to his beloved Fanny Brawne. His "bright star," who delighted and exasperated him in equal measure. The woman stolen from Keats by poverty and death. Lena read Ben's poem slowly, luxuriously, letting the words grow roots inside her body and wrap flowered vines around her broken heart.

For my dearest Lena,

We promised each other a life of romance to make our literary heroes jealous. Keats, Shelley, and Bryon. Our love will eclipse them all. We won't succumb to tragedy's early frost or grow old and grey and listless. You and I will be like nature: beautiful, unpredictable and ever changing.

In spring, I'll twist apple blossoms into your long hair; in summer, I'll capture cool breezes to caress your hot skin. In fall, we'll sleep on piles of red-gold leaves; and in winter, I'll gather snowflakes, each one precious, unique and lay them at your feet.

If we should ever become separated, return to the place where our two souls became one. Never fear, I'll find you again. My final and truest vow. True romantics are never parted.

She returned to the Lake District the very next day. Despite the passing of twenty years, Lena was able to retrace her and Ben's path through the woodland with ease. She could still hear the echo of their footsteps and the sound of their laughter mingling with the breeze. When she came to the place where she and Ben had made their vows, she stood as still and silent as the surrounding trees. She closed her eyes and breathed in deeply letting the sounds of nature wash over her. The wind rustled through the grass; birds sang; water rippled over earth and stone. She listened to it all, remembering, and just when she thought she could bear it no more she heard Ben's voice calling her name.

She opened her eyes and saw Ben standing beside an ancient Dalston oak. The outline of his body was hazy and indistinct, but she would know him anywhere. The curve of his shoulder; the narrow slant of his hips; and of course, the widow's peak that her fingers longed to caress. Everything the same and yet somehow different. She could see the outline of the treetops on his torso, and his eyes had taken on a deeper green, echoing the deep vermillion of the moss-covered rocks beneath her feet. Ben called her name a second time and held out his arms. The forest held its breath while Lena ran towards Ben and collapsed into his embrace. Like true romantics they held each other at arm's length and stared into one another's eyes. They stayed that way for a long time before disappearing into the trees, never to be parted again.

The Best Man

JENNA ANDREWS

The bridal suite buzzed with excitement. Six bridesmaids, a hair stylist, a makeup artist and of course the bride, crowded into the hotel room amidst champagne and a great playlist.

"It's time to put on your veil," Rachel said.

The photographer snapped a few pictures as Rachel slipped the comb of the headpiece gently into her cousin's hair.

"You look incredible, Liv," Rachel said, trying to hold back tears. The veil fell softly like a whisper across Liv's shoulders, fanning out past her hips, draping behind her in a huge half circle. "It's exactly how I pictured you'd look."

"I can't believe that I'm getting married in just a few hours," Liv said. "It feels like yesterday that we were putting on pretend weddings in my backyard. Now it's the real thing."

A knock sounded at the door.

"I'll get that," Rachel said.

In the doorway stood an incredibly handsome

groomsman, balancing a tray piled high with sandwiches in one hand and a bridal bouquet in the other.

"Here let me help you," Rachel offered. The tray tipped, leaving the groomsman juggling both flowers and food. The bouquet slipped from his arms, and Rachel dove for it before the flowers hit the ground.

"Nice save. Do you play softball?" he joked.

Rachel was momentarily speechless. His eyes were distracting, deep blue like denim. "Once, maybe. I'm not really that good with anything that involves balls." Rachel regretted the words instantly. Heat crept up her cheeks. "Oh my god, did I just say that? I meant balls like tennis, soccer, you know what I mean."

"I know what you mean," he said, showing off a gorgeous dimple when he smiled. "But too bad, I'm really good at tennis and soccer."

Liv appeared in the doorway. "Hey Drew, I see you met my cousin, Rachel. What are you doing here? How's Gavin doing? Is his stomach acting up? Is he staying calm?"

"He's definitely having some anxiety, but he's really excited. Your bouquet was dropped off to our suite by mistake along with a tray of sandwiches. I volunteered to deliver it."

"Thanks," Liv said. "You better get back to him. You're the only person who can talk him down when he's getting nervous."

"Okay, okay, I'm going. Nice meeting you, Rachel."

"Same."

Rachel stepped back inside the bridal suite. Before she closed the door, she snuck one last glance at Drew before he disappeared down the hallway.

The next few hours flew by in a whirl of activity as Rachel, Liv and the rest of the bridesmaids smiled and posed for the camera. At half past four, a shiny white trolley pulled up outside the hotel and chauffeured the entire wedding party to the ceremony.

The drive to the venue was short, but the party inside was loud with laughter. Drum sounds blasted from the speaker. One of the groomsmen entertained the packed trolley with his TikTok rendition of "Renegade." Rachel couldn't help but bounce around in her seat, mimicking the infectious dance moves.

"He's pretty funny," Drew said as he changed seats and sat down next to Rachel.

"He's really good," she replied, scooting over toward the window, making room for him. "Damn, what happened to your boutonniere?" A mangled white rose and a sprig of green hung limply from Drew's lapel.

"Collision course with my granddad. He hugged me a little too hard back at the hotel."

Drew pulled the pearl headed pin from his lapel. "Do you think anyone will notice if I don't wear one?"

"Yes, but I can help." Rachel pulled a rose from the back

of her bouquet and threaded the pin through the stem and the sprig of green. "Turn toward me." Rachel took hold of Drew's jacket and lifted the lapel, inserting the pin from the back, making sure that she didn't poke him. She swore that she could feel his heart beating just beneath her hand. "Looks pretty good."

"Thanks," Drew said. "So how come we've never met?"

"I've been working in LA for the past couple of years. I just moved back to Philly a few months ago."

"I live in West Chester."

"The suburbs?" Rachel said, a little more exaggerated than intended.

"Hey, what's wrong with the suburbs?" he asked.

"Nothing." She gave a little laugh. "I just prefer the busyness of a city, having tons of restaurants close by and being able to walk everywhere."

"Yeah, I miss being able to walk home from a bar. But I foster dogs, and I need space for them to run. I have four at home with a dog sitter right now."

"You foster dogs? That's awesome!" Rachel said. "I volunteer at the Second Chance shelter on weekends."

"I know them. They do great work!"

Rachel was about to launch into a story about their most recent rescue, but the trolley rolled to a stop outside Chandler Hall. A grand Victorian mansion perched on the water's edge, surrounded by tall maples with a spacious green lawn that unfolded down to a sugary white beach.

"Wow! This place is incredible," Rachel said.

"It is."

"Yo, Drew." A groomsman called from the front of the trolley. "We gotta go."

Drew reluctantly got up from his seat. "Thanks for the flower. Guess I'll see you out there," he said, finally making his way out of the trolley with the rest of the groomsmen.

Rachel glanced out the window. She could pick Drew out of the group even from behind. Rachel was looking forward to talking to him again. He was friendly and really good looking.

Catching up with him again would have to wait though. The wedding planner had just boarded the trolley and was motioning for the bride and bridesmaids to exit.

Soft music filled the air. Rachel fluffed Liv's gown and veil one last time, before she proceeded down the aisle. A hauntingly sweet instrumental version of "Jar of Hearts" played, sending a chill down Rachel's spine.

She looked up and found Drew's eyes on her. He stood next to his brother, Gavin, at the end of the runner under a white gazebo embellished with pampas grass, green tipped white hydrangeas and baby's breath. He didn't look away. She took a deep breath, suddenly self-conscious, praying that she didn't trip on the runner. Instead, she focused on the pearl blue sky, the tall maples whose leaves rustled in the soft breeze drifting gracefully to the ground and the blue-brown ocean painted across the landscape.

Drew smiled as she got closer. His eyes seemed even bluer in the sunlight.

The music shifted. Liv began her walk down the aisle in a cloud of tulle, pearls and lace. Butterflies swirled in Rachel's stomach, and she convinced herself Liv's happiness was the reason as she took her place beside the other bridesmaids.

The short ceremony passed in a blur. Vows were made. Rings were exchanged. And then Gavin was kissing his bride. Cheers of congratulations and applause greeted the couple as they moved past the wedding guests and headed to the Grand ballroom.

Rachel and Drew followed close behind. When she tried to pull away at the end of the aisle, he held onto her hand. She knew he held on as the best man to her maid of honor, and she threaded her fingers through his—surprised at how natural it felt—and let herself be led into the mansion. Her first glimpse of the ballroom left her speechless. The room glowed with thousands of twinkling lights that gracefully draped across the dance floor. Lush festoons of flowers adorned a winding staircase. It reminded Rachel of a scene from Bridgerton.

"I'll get us drinks," Drew said.

"Thank you. A vodka club, extra lime, please."

Soon the rest of the wedding party, including the bride and groom, crowded in around her. When Rachel saw Drew headed back with the drinks, she met him halfway.

"Let me help you," she offered, taking her drink from his

hand.

"Looks like the entire wedding party has caught up to us," Drew said. "Let's hang here."

"This venue is magical. I had no idea it even existed. My family spent all of our summers in Cape May, but we never made it this far south."

"Same. My parents rented a home every summer on Lafayette Street."

"Seriously?" Rachel asked. "Mine too. We could have been on the same beach together as little kids."

"I think I remember you. Were you the freckled girl with braids who was constantly feeding the seagulls?" Drew's tone was light.

Rachel laughed. "No way. I'm actually afraid of birds. All kinds, seagulls, blue jays, parrots…you name it. I don't like them."

It was Drew's turn to laugh. "Well, I like birds. Especially eagles. The kind that play football."

"Oh, here we go, another ball that I can't seem to catch. Don't hold it against me. I have no problem watching sports. I actually like going to the games. I'm just not that good at playing them."

"You're funny, and you're really easy to talk to," Drew said. "I'd—"

"Hey, you guys, quit being so anti-social." Liv took hold of Rachel's arm and pulled her over to the rest of the wedding party. Rachel glanced back at Drew, wishing he had gotten the chance to finish his sentence. "The band is getting ready to start and we need to hit the dance floor," Liv said.

True to her word, Liv and Gavin opened the dance floor with their first dance, "Perfect," by Ed Sheeran. Soon they invited the rest of the wedding party to join them, and Rachel felt Drew's hand envelope hers. Strong arms wrapped around her. Rachel moved closer, fitting her body close to his. It felt natural, like she had danced with him a thousand times before. His scent was intoxicating, woodsy with a touch of vanilla.

"You smell good," he whispered close to her.

Rachel looked up at him and smiled. "I was just thinking the same thing about you." The song ended, and reluctantly they separated as the band broke into a livelier Motown set. After five quick songs, the band leader invited the wedding party and their guests to take their seats. It was time for the speeches.

The toasts began with the father-of-the bride. Drew was up next. He stood nonchalantly with one hand in his pocket, the other holding a flute of champagne. Strong arms sculpted the lines of his jacket, but it was his blue eyes that Rachel was so drawn too. During their one slow dance, she noticed that his eyes glinted with mischief when he joked, but other times, they turned an even deeper shade of blue. She felt a sense of excitement when she gazed into their depths.

Her last relationship had ended on good terms, and she'd been glad to live on her own for a while, but recently she'd been feeling the loss. She missed having someone to hold her. Maybe it was time to start something new.

The maître d' handed Drew a microphone. "For those who don't know me, I'm Drew, Gavin's brother. It's an honor to stand here as his best man, to welcome you, to share this perfect night."

Rachel got caught up in the moment: the beautiful couple, the handsome best man, the fairy-tale setting of the venue. It was incredibly romantic. Her mind drifted, and she couldn't help thinking about what her own wedding would look like one day. Applause and laughter from the wedding guests pulled her back to the present.

Drew was wrapping up his speech. "A huge thank you to Liv and my brother for being the ultimate inspiration for all of us singles out here."

Rachel couldn't be sure, but she thought Drew looked straight at her when he said that last line.

"Please raise your glass and toast our newlyweds Olivia and Gavin St. Thomas."

Rachel lifted her flute with the rest of the wedding guests, feeling nostalgic and hopeful for the future.

The wedding reception moved quickly into the cool evening. Rachel was having the best time. Drew remained close, dancing with her and the other bridesmaids, but mostly Rachel. She had been to countless weddings over the past couple of years, but Liv and Gavin's was simply the most fun by far.

"I could use a break and a bottle of water," Rachel yelled over the band. Drew pointed to an outdoor area set up with a bar, sofas and chairs.

"I forgot to mention that your best man's speech was awesome," she said, once they got outside.

"Thanks. I was a little nervous. I didn't want to disappoint Gavin."

"I'm pretty sure I saw him smiling."

"Good. My first speech was longer and full of crazy stories. When I read it back, it didn't sound all that funny. I decided to make it more about Gavin and Liv and less about all the trouble we got ourselves into in high school and college."

"I think that was smart, more mature anyway."

"Rachel, can I see your phone?"

"Why?"

"I'd like to—holy shit! Is that smoke?"

The sound of an alarm pierced the air. Black smoke billowed from inside the building. Rachel stood frozen, in shock, not knowing what to do. Drew ran back inside. She tried to follow him, but a wall of chaotic, screaming wedding guests blocked her way.

Sirens wailed in the distance. Where was Drew? Where was Liv? Oh my god! What was happening? She tried to remain calm, but she was so scared. She stood stunned where Drew had left her, wanting to help but not knowing how. Bridesmaids and groomsmen ran from the building. Finally, Liv, Gavin and Drew sprinted through the door. Liv had lost a shoe and her gown was torn. Gavin was bleeding from a cut on his forehead and his once-white tuxedo shirt was streaked black.

A fire crew arrived. A long hose snaked around the mansion. "Is everyone out?" the fire captain yelled.

Liv coughed. "I don't know. You can't see anything in there. There's so much smoke."

"What happened to Gavin?" Rachel asked, helping all three.

"It was hard to see in there, and he got trampled trying to get Liv and some older folks out," Drew said.

"Bro, thanks for coming back in for us."

A second fire company arrived as the first trolley pulled away. The ride back to the hotel was dismally sullen. Rachel couldn't help but feel cheated, and she felt so guilty about that. This wasn't her. There were no contingencies on fate. Her guilt suddenly turned to sadness. Sorrow for the venue that caught on fire, and for Liv and Gavin having something like this happen on their very special day. Of all the mishaps that could come from a wedding, no one expected a kitchen fire to encompass the building.

The trolley lurched to a stop. Guests shuffled out and made their way into the hotel. Rachel, Liv and Gavin were the last to get off. She looked around for Drew but didn't see him. She hoped that he had gotten on the next trolley.

The overcrowded lobby buzzed with activity as people rehashed the night's turn of events. Some headed for the hotel bar. Rachel helped Liv and Gavin into the elevator and was about to follow them when she heard her name.

"Hey Rach."

She turned to see Drew off to the side of the lobby. The two buttons of his shirt were undone and his bow tie hung loose around his neck. "Wanna go for a walk?"

Drew led Rachel past the hotel bar and out into the night. The beach was dark. No moon, no stars, just a gray lining of clouds stretched across a dark slate sky.

Darkness enveloped them with the smell of sea salt heavy in the air. Gentle waves lapping at the shore was the only sound that could be heard for miles. Drew moved closer.

"I have to be honest, I was a little freaked out when you ran back into the fire."

"I just reacted. My family was in there."

"Mine too, but I just froze. You were incredibly brave."

"Incredibly brave or incredibly stupid," Drew said, "I just realized how bad I stink of smoke."

"You're fine, it's nice actually," she joked, "sooty with a touch of campfire."

He laughed, but then turned serious and reached for her, lowering his head. He lingered for a second, his lips hovering above hers, before his mouth dipped down, capturing hers in a slow kiss.

His hand gently curled around her neck. His lips parted hers, his tongue gently pushing inside Rachel's mouth.

She wavered unsteadily as the kiss became more intense. He pulled her closer, molding his body into hers. Rachel sighed and smiled when they parted.

Never had she experienced so many emotions in one day: joy, excitement, shock, disappointment, desire. Drew kissed her neck, finding that exact spot that sent shivers down her spine.

"Are you cold?" he asked, removing his jacket and draping it over her shoulders.

Rachel moved closer and rested her head against his chest. She could feel his heart beat as he wrapped his arms around her, keeping her warm. It felt natural to be here, within his arms, and that's when she realized that this could turn into something more.

"Hey Rach, let me see your phone?"

Her cell phone came to life as Drew entered his number. "I'd like to get together again. You could drive out to the suburbs," he said with enough exaggeration to make her laugh, "and meet the dogs."

Rachel took her phone back and immediately sent him a text message, then wrapped her arms around his neck, pulling him closer until their lips met.

Shark Out of Water

JANICE RIDER

The sun felt warm on my arms and face. As I sat on the sand on Kawela Beach along the North Shore of Hawaii, I envied other young people around me. They had bare legs as well as bare arms. The scars on my legs are obvious and ugly. After my surgeries, I did try wearing shorts; however, the gapes, gasps and looks of horror were too much for me to bear. Before the accident, I surfed competitively. Surfing is a dangerous sport. Jellyfish, riptides, rogue waves, aggressive surfers and leash tangles all pose risks. There is even the remote possibility of running into a shark. It was a belligerent surfer who ended my career by stealing my wave and forcing me onto some coral. My legs were badly cut up. Swimming into shore, I left a trail of blood in the water, which made me fearful that a shark would find me. As it turned out, that didn't happen, at least, not then.

Further down the beach, I saw a tall, muscular young man approaching. I sighed and closed my eyes. Maybe he would leave me alone. Moments later, a deep male voice accosted me, "Fabia, want to see me surf some waves?"

Reluctantly, I peered up at the youthful Adonis hovering over me. He had dark curls and long lashes framing hazel eyes. My friend, Vasilisa, couldn't understand why I wasn't crazy about him.

"Tamir," I responded, "I want to see you get caught in the next riptide!"

"No way, Girl! You don't mean that! Tell me for true, am I handsome?"

I shrugged. "You'll do."

"I'll do? I cut a dash! I am the big fish! With me in your life, you'd have a whale of a time!"

"Ha!" I retorted. "With you in my life, I'd want a sea change!"

Now, jogging down the beach from the opposite direction, my friends, Vasilisa and Pakpao, appeared. Vasilisa is all enthusiasm and impulsivity, but she is fun to be with and up for anything; in sharp contrast, Pakpao is well thought out and cautious. I trust Pakpao's judgment; she is the one I turn to when I require a sounding board. Vasilisa was interested in Tamir and had been for some time. It was a shame that he was focused on the wrong woman.

Pulling up beside us, Vasilisa exclaimed, "Tamir, you're looking great!"

Pakpao halted behind Vasilisa and rolled her eyes and said, "Quit pulling his leg and telling him whatever he wants to hear!"

"You girls are late," I reprimanded my friends before gesturing to Tamir with a thumb. "I had to put up with this guy for a full three minutes."

"A painful experience," Pakpao said, "and something that no one should have to suffer."

"I don't mind spending time with you, Tamir," Vasilisa reassured my admirer.

Rising to my feet and then my toes, I looked Tamir in the eye and said, "There you go! I bet if you asked Vasilisa to watch you surf, she'd be happy to do so."

"And where are you going?" Tamir inquired.

"Shopping."

"I'll surf some other time then." With those words, Tamir wandered off down the beach, checking out all the skin on display as he passed sunbathers.

"That man is so arrogant and self-satisfied, he makes me nauseous," Pakpao commented.

Vasilisa frowned. "It must be hard to be humble when you're that well-proportioned."

"It's not even noon, and already the sun is frying her brain," Pakpao told me as she shook her head from side to side in mock alarm. "Let's shop!"

When our shopping expedition was over, my friends and I settled into a cafeteria not far from the sea. Predictably, Vasilisa was the only one who had purchased anything. We chatted about our parents and siblings, mutual friends and guys, the sea and boats. It was when we had run out of things to talk about and were sitting in companionable silence that

Tamir blew through the door looking disheveled and distraught. Upon seeing us, he stumbled in our direction, braced himself on our table with one hand, and gasped out, "I decided to ride my board after all. I was charging in on a wave, preparing to take air, and feeling really amped when, all of a sudden, there, beneath me, I saw a monstrous form - a shark! Fear enveloped me from head to toe. I had a dark vision of my own…" At this point, Tamir stopped to catch his breath.

"Death, perhaps," Pakpao suggested.

"No, not that! Far worse!"

"Worse than death? Really?" I asked.

"Yes, I imagined uglification, great chunks of myself missing. I even had a brief moment when an image flashed through my mind of girls on the beach turning away from me and exclaiming in horror!"

"No girl would ever do that!" Vasilisa attempted to comfort him, gently patting his hand.

Engrossed in his story, it was as if Tamir hadn't heard her. "I knew I had to stay on my board. I couldn't afford to wind up in the soup! My talent, technique and tremendous desire to avoid the scar marks of predatory teeth saw me to land and salvation."

I began to clap and was soon joined by Pakpao and Vasilisa. Pakpao and I clapped slowly and dramatically, intimating that we thought Tamir was attempting to pull one over on us, again. Vasilisa applauded with genuine warmth. "You," I told Tamir, when we tired of clapping, "are a consummate schemer and tale teller."

It was then that I first saw him, a slender, graceful figure stepping through a window of the cafeteria. "This man is telling you the truth," he said, blue eyes catching the light from the ceiling of the restaurant in a way that accentuated their depth.

"There was a shark?" I asked.

"Oh yes, a large one, quite a magnificent sight," the stranger said, his eyes boring into mine.

"You actually saw it?" Pakpao interrogated him, suspicion in her voice.

"I was in the water at the time. Swimming."

"You seem calm for someone who was in the water with a shark. Isn't Tamir's response more logical?" Pakpao continued.

"I'm not afraid of sharks. Never have been."

"You must be brave," I said, feeling as I spoke these words, an attraction to the stranger.

Tamir glared at the man, no doubt jealous. "It's more likely that this guy is missing some marbles."

The blue eyes slid over to Tamir, and it seemed to me that as they did, they became more slate gray in color. "I must warn you not to sail in uncharted seas. You don't know me."

"Know that I am a real man," Tamir boasted, standing tall and thrusting his chin forward.

The newcomer looked Tamir up and down. "You do look like one," he responded.

"Did you see how I landed on the beach?" Tamir snarled

defensively.

Smiling, the stranger said, "Head up, feet down! Well done!"

Tamir nodded his head. "Exactly! I bailed at just the right moment! These gals would have been impressed, don't you think?"

"I was, and you took off at an impressive gallop right after you landed!"

At this, Pakpao and I laughed. Vasilisa scowled at the two of us and intervened with a question. "Who are you?"

"Mano is my name," the stranger said.

"Well, Mano," Tamir said in a scornful voice, "we should inform the Coast Guard about the shark."

"No need. The shark is gone." Mano spoke with authority.

"You don't know that! That gray demon could return at any time!"

"He could not," insisted Mano.

"How can you be certain?" I asked.

"I know sharks," the stranger replied.

Pakpao, who had been silently cogitating, now stood, the light of certainty and knowledge in her eyes. "You're an ichthyologist, aren't you?"

Confusion clouded Tamir's face, a not infrequent occurrence. "Icky what?"

"Ichthyology is the study of bony, cartilaginous and jawless fish," Pakpao informed us.

Mano nodded in validation of the information Pakpao had bequeathed us. "I have studied fish and found many of them to be very tasty."

Pakpao snorted, a definite sign of amusement. "Well, Mano, you may know a lot about sharks and other fish, but for once I agree with Tamir. The Coast Guard should be notified. Sharks are potentially dangerous."

The next day I was down on a pier. To my surprise, I saw Mano striding in my direction, a shy smile on his face. He wasn't as tall as Tamir, but his muscles were lean and sculpted. His hair was shaved right down to his scalp, giving him a tough, sleek look, and his blue eyes radiated magnetism. I felt a frisson of expectation run through my body. Mano arrived at my side and stared out onto the water with me. He didn't speak. Curiosity got the better of me. "What do you see?"

"I see variations on a blue theme. In spite of my familiarity with the ocean, I am always amazed at the fact that blue is so much more than one identifiable hue. What do you see?"

This fellow was unusual. Forget about idle chit chat. I pondered my answer and decided on a version of the truth. "My destiny. A silly thing to say, perhaps, but I enjoy the play of wind and sun on water."

He smiled then, revealing white, white teeth. "I like your answer."

"Are you on a holiday? I don't believe you live around here."

"Oh, I live around here, but I'm not from Oahu."

"Another island, then?"

"No. I came here to meet you."

Involuntarily, I drew back from Mano. I have never liked forward men, which was part of the reason Tamir rubbed me the wrong way. My reaction elicited an unexpected response. Mano pulled away from me as if he had been stung. "I have offended you. I am so sorry."

"I'm not offended, but I am surprised at your boldness."

"There are two kinds of surprises–wonderful ones, the kind where you spot a meal coming your way, for instance, and terrible ones, like the kind where you become someone else's meal."

"Well, I didn't think you were planning to eat me if that's any consolation."

Mano nodded as if my response was serious as opposed to facetious and moved off and away down the beach, leaving me to myself. I sighed, allowing my eyes to drift out to sea again.

Pakpao and Vasilisa have been friends with me since we were all young children. We all have genuine Hawaiian ancestry in our genes, which is why our parents gave us Hawaiian names. As a result of our long-standing friendship, I have difficulty in pulling the wool over my friends' eyes. They noticed that I was more distracted and distant than usual after Mano and I were on the pier together. Pakpao came to the point immediately. "You're enamored, Fabia. I've never seen you like this before."

"Bosh!" I protested. "I'm thoughtful. You see, I've been considering whether or not I should pursue a master's degree after I graduate."

"Nonsense!" Vasilisa exclaimed. "No master's degree fills a person's eyes with constellations. Say, if you love Mano, I can have Tamir!"

"The question is: Will he have you?" Pakpao inquired.

"There's not much point in him continuing to pine for Fabia."

"When has something being pointless ever stopped Tamir from doing it? Pursuing Tamir is a waste of your time," I told Vasilisa.

"Fabia is correct. In matters of love, however, it is the one whose heart has been stolen who can't think or see straight. You, Fabia, like Vasilisa, are not thinking rationally," Pakpao said with an air of righteous superiority, "so you should consider these words of advice. You need to be cautious in regard to Mano. We know nothing about him. And remember, I have enough work to do keeping Vasilisa out of trouble. I don't want to have to ensure that you don't come to grief, too."

Vasilisa made a dismissive, impertinent sound and waved in Pakpao's direction as if shooing away a mosquito. "Perhaps Mano has a deep, dark past," she speculated, wiggling her fingers dramatically. "His father is a politician, and his mother is a lawyer."

We all laughed then, and I felt the familiar warmth of our togetherness as something solid and unshakeable. Later in the afternoon, we sauntered to the beach and were surprised to see Tamir there with Mano. As we drew closer from behind the two of them, we heard Tamir instructing Mano in the art of surfing. I have to admit, Tamir does have expertise in this area.

"So, surfing is the way to impress women," Mano said. "What if I body surfed? It's what I'm used to doing."

"Mano, my man, girls love a guy with a board!" Tamir responded, shaking his head at Mano's naivety. "They want to see you take air, carve and cross step." As his last sentence was met with a blank look, Tamir explained. "When your surfboard leaves the water, it's called taking air. Carving is turning on a wave. As for cross stepping, that's when you run on the surfboard as it moves through the water. Surfing will make you feel like a man!"

"Is there something that would make you think I'm not a man?"

"Buddy, looking manly isn't enough. Jump up on my board." Mano leapt lightly onto Tamir's surfboard. "Right. Now, bend your knees, lean forward and put your arms out front and back. Looking good! Assume an expression of confident machismo."

"Machismo?" Mano inquired.

"Yeah. You need to look powerful and bold. And smile."

Mano bared his white, white teeth. Tamir smacked a palm

to his forehead. "You look like you're about to devour something, Bro! You don't want to scare people, especially not those of the opposite sex."

"It's my default face!" Mano explained.

Tamir caught sight of us at this point and grinned broadly. Gesturing to Mano, he said, "This guy's never surfed on a board! Can you believe it?"

Embarrassed, Mano turned to me and asked, "Do you surf?"

"I used to," I replied.

"Fabia surfed competitively!" Vasilisa declared with fervent loyalty and pride. "She was the best of the best!"

One of Mano's eyebrows arched upwards. "Why don't you surf anymore?"

I shrugged like it was no big deal. "I'm no longer interested." It was a lie, of course. I used to love the feeling of riding a wave. Waves are a force of nature and being on top of one is liberating. When I recalled taking air on my surfboard, that sensation of soaring, I felt a sadness that threatened to overwhelm me. I turned and walked away. Vasilisa bolted after me, but Pakpao charged after her and steered her clear of me, knowing I needed some time alone.

It was Mano who found me on the pier where we'd met some days earlier. Had I gone to the same pier in the hope that he would seek me out? Perhaps. Once again, he came up beside me and simply stood there scanning the water. I appreciated the fact that he was quiet. We stood for some time. Finally, I initiated a conversation. "The waves were unpredictable and fierce that day. I was injured when an aggressive surfer forced me off my board and onto some coral. I thought sharks would find me and eat me. My legs are a mess. The other surfer never even bothered checking to see if I was all right."

Turning towards me, Mano nodded his head in understanding. "You are afraid."

"Of course."

"Would you enter the water with me? I'm not talking about going far. We could wade and splash up to our knees."

"How about if I sit on the pier and watch you swim?" I countered.

Mano leapt off the end of the pier immediately, still in his shorts and t-shirt, entering the water with smooth elegance. I sat to watch him swim. He moved in the sea as if he'd been swimming since birth. Agile and quick, powerful and graceful, he turned swimming into an art form. Finally, he dove deep and propelled himself to the surface with sufficient force to launch himself high enough to grip the pier and pull himself back onto it. Water splashed off his body onto my bare arms, my head and my face. I shivered and closed my eyes. When I opened them, Mano was close, his blue eyes drinking me in. "May I kiss you?" he asked, his voice rough with emotion.

"Yes," I whispered. When he leaned in and touched his lips to mine, I tasted salt water. His kiss was tender, even tremulous, and he broke off before I wanted him to, for this man awakened a yearning in me that I had never felt before, a yearning and a vulnerability.

"Well," I said, abruptly, "it's time for me to head home."

Hurt swam through Mano's eyes just long enough for me to see it, and then he sighed, dropping his gaze. "Yes, I guess I should be going, too."

As he turned to leave, his sodden t-shirt stretched over his chiseled muscles, I spoke. "Mano, would you like to meet here again tomorrow? Maybe late in the afternoon? Say, around four?"

Mano's head swiveled. His eyes were lit well down into their depths. "I would."

That's how it began. We were together most days after that, as soon as I had finished with my studies in marine biology, and he had finished at the local aquarium, which was excited to hire someone with an extensive personal knowledge of marine creatures. Soon, I was wading and swimming in the water. Eventually, I even got back on my surfboard, baring my legs to the world. The scars on my limbs didn't disgust Mano. He never even flinched the first time he saw them. "Your legs are part of you," he said, "and that makes them beautiful." With Mano beside me, I braved people's stares and found myself comfortable with their discomfort.

Vasilisa was delighted for me, but Pakpao was full of doubts. Again and again, my cautious friend counseled me against putting my trust in someone who wasn't forthcoming enough to reveal his past. As for Tamir, he went from courting Mano's friendship to glowering whenever he spotted

Mano with me. I was astonished that Tamir was interested in me after seeing my legs. It made me begin to think his interest was genuine.

At this time, there was an announcement for the famous Aqua Triple Crown of Surfing at Pipeline Beach. For the first time ever, women would be competing against men in this event. Tamir planned to vie for one of the monetary prizes, and Mano encouraged me to do so too. Vasilisa and Pakpao also put pressure on me to enter the contest, but Tamir was the reason I actually signed on as a competitor. He overheard my friends badgering me and had the gall to remark, "There's no way any woman can beat a man at the sport of surfboarding. Let Fabia alone!"

"You think I can't beat you at a sport that makes me feel more alive than almost anything else I know of?" I asked, practically spitting the words out into Tamir's face.

"I'm the big fish, remember?" Tamir teased me. "You should have stuck with me, Girl, instead of going for that loser, Mano."

"The biggest fish aren't always the fastest or the most agile, Mister," I reminded him. "And guess what? I am entering the Aqua Triple Crown of Surfing, and I plan to win one of the prizes. I will certainly do better than you!"

Tamir gave me a lopsided grin. "Good luck. You're going to need it."

For the next couple of weeks, I practiced surfboarding every single day. Mano swam close by while I honed my techniques. My confidence grew daily. One day, following a lot of time out on the water, I made time to see my friends. We went back to the little cafeteria near the sea and were enjoying ourselves over some sushi, when Tamir interrupted us in the middle of our meal. The man crashed through the door of the cafe causing me to jump. I almost aspirated fish into my lungs and was forced to cough violently to prevent my own suffocation. When I recovered, Tamir bellowed, "Girls, I've got some seriously bad news!"

Pakpao spoke with scorn. "You have a pimple burgeoning in the center of your forehead or something?"

"What's your news, Tamir?" Vasilisa queried. "I'm all ears!"

"Ears, eyes and tail," Pakpao scoffed, "just like a puppy!"

"It's Mano. Every morning he rises early and heads down to the sea."

"Oh, no!" I pretended to panic. "We have an early riser amongst us! How did you find out? Isn't your normal waking time about noon?"

"Let me continue. Mano swims out to sea."

"He's an excellent swimmer. It's not smart to swim alone, but, in the water, the man's a fish," Vasilisa reassured Tamir.

"Yes!" Tamir exclaimed. "That's exactly what he is, and, having done my homework for the first time in my life, I can tell you he's a cartilaginous one!"

Pakpao was brimming with annoyance by this time. "You're not particularly easy to understand at the best of times, and this is not the best of times for you. Why don't you condense your dissertation into a digestible amount for us?"

"Mano's the shark that was under my board the first day we met him. He's a tiger shark!"

Vasilisa rarely flared, but she did that day. "You're saying this because you're still interested in Fabia! Listen, Buddy, she couldn't care less about you! Making this stuff up is crazy! What's more," and here she rose to her feet, "you've got someone right here, right now, staring you in the face who does care about you!"

"I'm telling the truth, Girls. Meet me down on the beach at the umbrella stand at four thirty tomorrow morning." Tamir turned and bolted out the cafeteria door.

"Four thirty?" Vasilisa blanched and folded back into her seat. "Fabia, you and Pakpao will have to carry me down to the beach. Why did I give my heart to someone so determined to love another?"

"This is utter nonsense," Pakpao muttered. "There must be something else going on."

I had told Mano that when I looked out at the sea, I saw my destiny. Mano's facility in the water made him seem a part of it, and his intimate knowledge of marine life was uncanny. Pakpao was correct. Something was going on. I shivered.

Next morning, having met Tamir at the umbrella stand, we made our way to some vegetation across from the broad curve of Kawela Bay. It wasn't long before we saw a dorsal fin moving towards the shoreline. A shark! When the creature reached the shallows, its fins became arms and the dorsal fin sank down into its back. Mano rose out of the water, a mythic beast come to life, just like the son of the shark king in ancient Hawaiian mythology. A scream rang out! I realized I was the one screaming. I hadn't fallen in love with a man! Mano was some kind of dangerous predator, a wereshark or something! Why hadn't I listened to Pakpao?

Mano's head spun in our direction when he heard me scream. Upon seeing me, his face crumpled, and he headed toward us. Unable to bear the thought of him getting close, I fled as fast as my legs could carry me. Behind me, I heard his voice calling, "Fabia, wait! love you!"

When I flashed a glance over my shoulder, Mano was running, too, but he wasn't running after me, he was running back to the sea.

In times of trouble, I always seek out my grandmother. Her lustrous, black hair has turned gray, but her eyes are still dark and wise. On the day that I found out what Mano was, I went to visit her.

"My dear," she said in a bright voice as I barged through her door, "how good it is to see you! That young man of yours is absorbing much of your time. I was almost worried you'd forgotten me."

"He's a shark," I wept.

"A shark? Oh, that is bad. A loan shark or a card shark? I think that if I had to choose between them, I'd choose the card shark. A man who's clever with cards is intriguing."

"Mano's the kind of shark who swims in the ocean."

I thought my grandmother would think I'd gone nuts. Instead, she took in my words with a serious expression. "Why, of course, I should have known. That's why he smells so much like the sea! And come to think of it, Mano is the Hawaiian word for shark. Fascinating!"

"Do you want your one and only granddaughter to be eaten by a shark?"

Taking my hands, my grandmother asked, "Has Mano ever tried to nibble on you before?"

I paused before responding. "Not so as to leave any marks."

"And don't you love him?"

"I used to."

"Ah. You loved your story about Mano, the mysterious stranger who came into your life and helped bolster your confidence. You don't love the real Mano. I understand."

"He's a shark!"

"Well, it's too bad you found out about that because now he knows that your love is only skin deep."

"Grandmother! I'm feeling hurt."

"I'm sure Mano is feeling hurt, too."

"He's returned to the ocean. I'll never see him again."

"Child, he won't miss the Aqua Triple Crown, not with you in the competition. Compete! He'll be there!"

"Fabia Malona! Fabia Malona!" My name rang out on the lips of the crowd around me again and again. It felt fantastic to have done so well on my board, riding a huge, powerful wave to shore with the wind in my hair. Out on the water, I felt exhilaration and a deep sense of connection to the ocean. My fear of surfing was gone. Now it was Tamir's turn to compete.

The voice of the announcer blared, "And now, we see Tamir Kama riding his surfboard with the ease of one who knows what he's about. This young daredevil is known as the Board Master and Board Master he is! He is up against stiff competition, though; Fabia Malona has proven to be a formidable contender."

The crowd went wild as we watched Tamir, shouting his name over and over. Suddenly, he disappeared from view, as if an invisible hand had snatched him from his perch. Silence descended as those of us on shore strained to see the young man with dark curls and hazel eyes. Suddenly, the distinct profile of a dorsal fin appeared, cleaving the water. Vasilisa wailed in fright.

"It's a shark!" the announcer bellowed. "Tamir is about to be eaten! Wait! The shark appears to be supporting him! Must be in preparation to devouring the poor fellow. Oh! There's the lifeguard motoring out! The shark has vanished! Tamir is being pulled from the water! This is a young man who will live to see another day!"

Tamir's audience went wild with joy. I felt my knees give way. Vasilisa whooped and flung her arms around Pakpao.

When Tamir stepped back on shore, he flashed a saucy grin at the cameras and said, "Lost my footing, and my board hit my head. Disoriented, I floundered in the briny deep. Then, in the nick of time, a shark out there pushed me to the surface! Fabulous specimen! Wasn't the least bit frightened, either."

The announcer shook his head sadly, "Tamir Kama is not yet in his right mind after a blow to the head, but let's hear it for his courageous sense of humor!"

The crowd whistled, cheered and roared, "Board Master, Board Master, Board Master!"

Tamir looked down at me then and winked. I knew in that moment he was letting me know that he would no longer be hanging around in my wake. I nodded to indicate that I understood.

Then, Tamir did something completely unexpected and out of character. He pointed to me and said, "Let's all applaud the real Board Master and the undisputed winner of the Aqua Triple Crown!" Once more, the crowd whistled, cheered and roared.

That night, Tamir and I were perched on the end of the pier under the light of a full moon, calling for Mano. A familiar form slid through the water. "Mano, is that you?" My voice quavered.

Mano burst through the sea's surface and latched onto the pier. Tamir shouted jubilantly, "Bro, you saved my life!"

"The two of you, together?" Mano asked, his eyes gray and sad.

"No way, man! I can't compete with you for Fabia's heart," Tamir declared. "I came to thank you for coming to my rescue when I came off my board. I swear no one shall learn of your secret from me ever again."

"And I've come to apologize for my reaction on the beach," I said. "I love you, Mano."

"I thought I was a thing you feared and loathed."

"I was afraid of you that day on the beach when I found out that you were a shark, but then I realized that it's the things under your skin that count. You didn't flee from me after you saw my legs. I shouldn't have run away from you, either."

Mano dove deep before launching himself onto the pier.

"You're some kind of man!" Tamir said in admiration. "Guess I'd better leave you two alone now."

"Guess you'd better," Mano agreed, his eyes only on me.

We kissed, then, and I tasted the sea on my lips.

Muffins and Meet-Cutes
SIMON QUINN

Seagulls squawked above me as waves crashed onto the sand next to me while I jogged down the beach. It was too early for the tourists to be out yet, and the sun was just starting to breach the horizon, but the cool air felt good against my sweat-slicked skin. Ever since I'd started jogging before work, I had fallen in love with the hour before sunrise. Watching the sunrise made the annoyance of interacting with customers at eight in the morning manageable.

"Watch out!" A voice interrupted my thoughts, and I stumbled, narrowly avoiding the easel in the middle of my path.

Except… how had I gotten so far off path? I liked running in the damp sand with the water running over my skin periodically, and now I was somehow up in the dry part where the driftwood and prickly dried seaweed stuck up waiting to be stepped on.

"Are you blind? You almost ran into me!" I focused on who was talking, only to find a guy with the most captivatingly gorgeous brown eyes glaring at me from behind the lenses of his round glasses.

I took out my earbuds and frowned. "I'm sorry, I wasn't paying attention."

"You almost took out my oil painting! I would have had to start from scratch," he grumbled, twisting back on his stool to face the easel again. "To think I got up at six am only for it to almost be for nothing."

I opened my mouth in indignation. I hadn't actually run into him, and he didn't need to be so rude about it.

Then he sighed, set his brush down on the lip of the easel and twisted to look at me. "I'm sorry, I'm just not a morning person."

"Then why not paint the sunset instead? Then you wouldn't be in the way of any more errant joggers," I said, albeit with more harshness in my voice than I meant there to be.

He shrugged. "The sunrise hurts my eyes less, plus the softer colors are more of a challenge to match."

I nodded like I understood and started to put my earbuds back in. "Okay, well good luck I guess. Maybe next time don't wait so long to give a warning." I left. I needed to get home and get ready for work.

I groaned as I heard the bells on the door jingle. It had been a nonstop flow of customers for the last four hours, and I just wanted to go home. My book was waiting for me to finish it while I laid in bed and let the world cease to exist.

I was too tired to scream, so instead I smiled as brightly as I could and turned toward the cash register to see a guy staring intently over my head at our menu.

"How can I help you?"

The guy on the other side of the counter jumped a little at my voice before taking out his earphones and smiling shyly at me.

Oh great. Was he going to hit on me?

"Ah, I'm sorry, I get startled easily. May I have a matcha latte and a chocolate muffin?" he asked as he dug out his wallet from his back pocket. "Also, forgive me if I'm overstepping, but aren't you the guy that almost ran into me this morning?"

"You didn't look so startled when you were yelling at me." I muttered as I typed the order into the tablet.

"Well maybe you missed it the same way you missed the entire easel."

I jerked my head up to see his smile widen just a bit. I narrowed my eyes. "That'll be seven forty-five. Cash or card?"

"What? No apology?" he joked as he pulled out his card.

I ignored him as I finished the transaction. I spun the tablet so he could sign and hopefully tip. "Did you want it to go or for here?"

"For here please."

"Okay. That'll be out in a bit."

"Thanks."

He sat at one of the high tables next to the big windows, pulled a notebook out of his bag and started writing intensely. Every so often he'd look out the window before looking back at the notebook.

"Zach, stop watching." My manager, Sarah, nudged my arm and nodded in his direction.

I frowned. "I'm not watching. I'm washing counters, see?" I waved the rag I was using at her.

She shook her head and went back to organizing the bags of coffee grounds under the counter.

After a while, he left and the rest of the day went on like normal. The sorority girls on summer vacation flirted with me like they always did, even though I didn't respond to it. The surfer bros wanting their smoothies tracked sand across the floor, that I would have to clean up later. Tourists with their sunburns always asked where I thought they should go next, not caring that I didn't know where they'd *been*. Of course there were also the people who would come in alone to sit at a table and look at their phone while drinking an espresso. People of all sorts left their empty cups and their napkins on their tables instead of picking up after themselves. Our designated dirty dish TSA airplane box that Sarah once stole for fun, seemingly invisible on its counter. Every day had its own monotony that not even the fresh sea breeze made better.

"Can I draw you?"

"Can I help you?" I grumbled, turning around to see the same guy from yesterday morning hiding behind his phone.

"Oh um, yeah, can I please have a matcha latte and a chocolate muffin?" He slipped his phone into his back pocket before pulling out his wallet. "And can I draw you?"

"Seven forty-five, and why would you want to draw me?" I took his card and swiped it through the machine.

"It's for one of my summer art classes. I'm supposed to do a candid figure study."

I handed back his card. "Aren't you not supposed to ask permission for candids? Like isn't the whole point that the subject doesn't know they're being used?"

Pink rose to color his cheeks as he coughed and rubbed the back of his neck. "Yeah, but I hate doing that. It makes me feel like I'm being rude. So I figured I'd ask first, but it's totally okay to say no! You don't know me after all."

I shrugged as I went to stick his muffin in the microwave. "It's fine with me. Not like I could stop you since I'm just stuck behind the counter all day."

"Thank you! I'll show you when I'm finished!"

I rolled my eyes at the microwave before plastering on the fake customer service smile and turning back around with the muffin. "You really don't have to do that."

"Oh but I want to! Since you agreed to be my model and all." He took the muffin and bit his lip for a moment before asking, "May I ask what your name is?"

"No you may not." I broke character and stuck my tongue out at him.

"Ah, okay, well uh thank you anyway and thank you for the muffin and the latte." He dipped his head, and his glasses slid down his nose a bit before he went to sit at a table that apparently had a better view of me since he kept looking up and then back down at his notebook.

"You're staring again." Sarah poked me in the side as she came up behind me.

I turned to her and leaned on the counter as best I could since it was much too short to lean down comfortably. "He asked to draw me."

"So I heard. Why did you say yes?"

I ran a hand through my hair and sighed. "He asked. Most people don't."

"Oh that's rich of you. You just wanted to see what would happen." She smirked before turning to make his latte. "Besides, you're in love with yourself."

"I am not!" I stood up and crossed my arms in indignation.

"Oh please, I've seen your camera roll. You have like three hundred selfies in there." She finished the latte and handed it to me. "Go take it to him."

"Those selfies are *documentation.* I have to see the change from when I started taking the man juice to now." I stuck my nose in the air.

"Oh please, Zach, it's been five years. You are in love with yourself, you need to admit it. Now go!" Sarah pushed my shoulder gently as the bells above the door jangled.

I took a deep breath to plaster on the fake smile again as I walked over to where he was sitting. "Here's your drink."

"Thanks!" he grinned up at me, and I blatantly ignored the way it looked adorable. I refused to be a part of a stupid meet-cute or whatever. Especially with someone who didn't understand that sometimes running in a straight line was too hard for a gay man.

"Yeah well you paid for it. Enjoy."

As I was walking back to the counter he shouted.

"My name's Jason!"

I spun on my heel to flip him off. "I don't care!"

He chuckled before taking a sip of his drink and going back to his notebook.

Unlike the day before, he *stayed*. The rest of the day went on with the routine that it always did, completely unaware that the entire structure of the shop was disrupted by the man sitting at the table one away from the counter who kept looking back and forth from me to his notebook. Well, I guess it was actually a sketchbook since that would make more sense for art? Ugh, I don't know. I couldn't deny that I had a *little* curiosity as to what I looked like through his pen, but I was not going to let him know that I wanted to actually see them.

"Um, I ordered a caramel latte and this is a peppermint one?"

I looked down at a girl that was standing across the counter and looking almost scared. She couldn't have been older than maybe sixteen.

"Oh, I'm sorry about that. I've been a little distracted today." I tried to smile in a way to ease her nerves, but I think I made it worse.

"Oh no it's okay, I'll just deal with it," she whimpered.

I opened my mouth to respond, to offer to replace it, but she scampered away back to a table with a laptop, backpack, and a very full binder. I watched as she took a sip and wrinkled her nose in disgust. I sighed, looked up to the ceiling for just a moment and remade the drink.

"Here, you ordered a caramel one and a caramel one you shall have." I placed the correct drink on her table. "Mind if I take the other one?"

She shook her head, and I scooped up the drink in one hand before walking over to Jason's table.

"This is your fault."

He jumped in his seat before looking up at me and pulling his sketchbook into his lap. "What is?"

I followed the motion of the sketchbook, and then let my gaze dance up his shirt to his neck and then finally his face. "Why did you hide the sketchbook?"

His lips quirked into a grin, and he leaned over the table, effectively covering the sketchbook in its entirety. "That's a different question."

I rolled my eyes in exasperation. "You are a thorn in my side."

"So what's my fault?"

I plunked the cup onto his table and gestured to it. "This."

"That…is a cup of coffee?"

"No. It is a peppermint latte that was supposed to be a caramel one, and because I have been distracted by you just sitting there and watching me all day, I messed it up. I never mess up."

He stared at me for a moment before bursting into giggles.

My cheeks flamed, but I ignored it.

"You really do care," he managed to get out between giggles.

"I do not!"

"You do. And you will see the sketchbook when I'm done with the sketches."

I glared at him before walking away with the cup. "Self-important asshole," I mumbled under my breath as I made it back behind the counter.

The day continued, but by that point all I wanted to do was to go home and watch a terrible movie with my cat. Sadly, there were still three hours left until closing, and *he* refused to leave. My irritability filtered through during my interactions with customers until Sarah told me to take a time out.

"You need to get your act together or go sit down until you can." She crossed her arms and raised an eyebrow at me.

"But I'm fine! I'm just a little tired, that's all."

"Go. Sit." She pushed me out, and I sighed in exasperation. "Maybe go join the person who's making you so distracted."

"What? But he—!"

She waved her hands at me, and I stuck my tongue out at her before turning to find a place to sit. Of course there weren't any tables left. Just my luck. I groaned and made my way over to Jason's table.

"Mind if I sit here?" I asked.

"Someone sounds grumpy," he joked, not looking up.

"Is that a yes or a no?"

He finally looked at me and opened his mouth in confusion. "Aren't you supposed to be working?"

I pulled out the chair opposite him and plopped down before saying in the chirpiest sarcastic voice I could muster. "You're not gonna believe this. A customer asked if he could draw me, and I agreed, and now he won't leave and my manager gave me a time out."

He chuckled, hiding his mouth behind the hand holding his pen. "I'm sorry?"

"You should be," I huffed.

He shrugged. "I mean, I don't really see how it's my fault. If you were going to be so distracted by me then why would you agree to it? You could have said no."

"I was curious."

"Impatient maybe."

"Do you always sketch in pen?"

He just stared at me for a moment, and I watched him back. "Uh, yeah. Makes sure I don't spend all my time erasing my work."

"That makes sense."

An awkward silence stretched between us before he cleared his throat and went back to sketching.

"Are you sure I can't see yet?" I asked.

He shook his head. "But I'm almost finished. Then you can see."

"Oh, okay."

I tried to wait, but the quiet between us sprawled across the table. I did my best to not let it intimidate me into talking again and instead let myself take him in. He had hung his jacket on his chair and his shirt was a deep purple that clung just close enough for me to appreciate that he didn't look horrible. Actually, he looked pretty okay. Maybe even good. Dark brown hair hung in waves around his face as his round glasses perched precariously on the end of his strong nose. One of his hands gripped his pen while the other held the sketchbook up at just the right angle to hide the page from me.

Okay fine. He was hot, and I was gay.

No one tell Sarah. I thought, making myself chuckle in the process.

He looked up at the sound, and I noticed that his eyes were a warm deep dark brown and that he maybe sort of potentially had a nice soft mouth that I might want to kiss. Maybe.

"Are you okay?"

"Just thinking." *I hate that I want to kiss you.* "Can I see yet?" I asked.

He bit his bottom lip as he glanced between me and his sketchbook, and I looked away quickly so he couldn't see that it was his fault that I wanted to hide under the table. He finally said, "Yeah, okay. I don't think I can make it any better." And then he slid it across the table, so I could finally see what he'd spent all day on.

"Holy shit," I murmured. That was me. That was *me* on that page. There were five sketches, all of me in different positions and of different parts of me. Me standing behind the register typing something in. Me making a drink. My hand resting on the back of a chair. The back of my head as I talked to a customer. Me leaning over the counter as I wiped it down.

"Did I do an acceptable job?"

"These are fantastic. You had better get a good grade or I'll sue your professor."

Jason laughed and I grinned as I looked up at him. He caught me looking and smiled a little brighter. "I'll take you up on that."

I squirmed in my chair as he watched me.

"Now may I know your name?"

"Uh, it's Zach. Why?" I frowned.

"So I can ask this?" He cleared his throat and smiled. "Will you go out with me, Zach?"

I stood up too fast and almost tripped over the leg of my chair. "I should really be getting back to work."

"Oh. Okay," he said, dejected. "Well I should get going."

"Jason?"

"Yeah?"

"I get off at six if you'd like to stick around?" I shrugged as I rubbed the back of my neck. "I can bring you another muffin. Maybe. If you would want. Or we could go get dinner after?"

He smiled. "All right then. Sounds like a plan."

I grinned as I walked back to my place behind the counter. Maybe it was okay that I participated in a meet-cute after all.

Wildwood
VALERIE HUNTER

Early mornings had become Florie's favorite time of day. The air still had a touch of coolness in it, and the streets were fairly quiet, just people like her hurrying to their jobs. It was the best time to get any kind of thinking done, though truth be told, Florie had been contemplating the same thing for a solid week and felt no closer to coming to a decision.

She touched the sharp corner of the letter in her pocket and wondered if it would have been easier to know her mind if Winfield had asked her in person. Her favorite brother had visited for the entire month of June, the first time they'd seen him since the war ended. He wasn't quite the same as Florie remembered, but that was to be expected—time changed everyone, and surely war did as well. She'd just been glad to see him, and he'd had a lovely visit before heading to Ohio and his new engineering job.

He'd sent the letter a month later, asking her to come live with him. He'd written all about his new home, how he had plenty of space, how he was more than happy to support her and the boys if she'd keep house for him.

She'd attempted to write a reply half a dozen times in the past week, but she couldn't seem to find the right way to phrase the innumerable questions that churned through her mind. Was Win actually lonely, or was he asking her out of pity? Did he realize that if she uprooted herself and her sons, she wanted permanence and stability? Suppose Win found a wife soon, what then? Of course he *should* find a wife, but what if she didn't get along with Florie, didn't want another woman in the house? Florie wouldn't blame this hypothetical future wife; a woman deserves her own home, without a sister-in-law and three nephews. On the other hand, suppose Win never married? Was being her brother's housekeeper meant to be her life's work? Did she want that?

It had been so long since she'd thought about *want* that it seemed a foreign concept. When Bill had disappeared on her, at the end of the summer of 1916, she'd been in a complete fog, had focused only on surviving, on keeping her sons housed and fed and clothed. She'd worked so hard to accomplish that, including through the two terrible years of war, that it seemed hard to believe that she'd succeeded.

If an offer like Win's had come three years ago, she'd have jumped at it. Now, when she had learned to make do for herself, when she no longer needed rescuing, it was an actual choice, and she wasn't sure what to do with it.

She loved Wildwood dearly, but the idea of a fresh start had allure. In Ohio she could call herself a war widow and leave it at that. Surely the pity that might evoke would be far more bearable than the terrible pity she was subject to now, poisoned as it was with blame and shame, that look behind people's eyes that asked what she'd done to make her husband up and leave her.

She hated that look, made worse by the fact that she had the same question. What *had* she done to make her husband leave in the dead of night without so much as a word or a note?

Realistically she knew she'd done nothing. She was a model housekeeper, a fine cook. The children were well cared for and well behaved. She never argued with Bill, never belittled him. Perhaps they weren't as romantic as in their courting days, but surely that was normal after eight years of marriage and three children?

What wasn't normal was abandoning your family, walking off with all your business's cash as well as the pin money your wife kept in the cookie jar. The sheer audacity of that made Florie wonder at first if Bill hadn't been kidnapped, or suffered a terrible injury that left him addle-headed. But no, this wasn't some dime novel. She'd been abandoned, betrayed, left behind like a threadbare towel on the beach.

And then she'd gotten a letter from Bill's mother at the end of the war telling Florie he'd died, and all the rage and betrayal that she had stowed away while she got on with surviving came back. She would never get to ask him why he'd done what he did. Never pour the full force of her anger over him. Never show him that she could get by all right without him.

Yes, a new start away from all that rage would be just the thing. So why couldn't she write and tell Win that?

Florie reached the Sea Crest Hotel and got on with her work cleaning the rooms. Wednesdays were her busiest days—the Sea Crest all morning, and five different houses to clean in the afternoon. Good money to be made now that the war was over, and the tourists were back in full force.

By the time she left the last house, the afternoon sun was blazing, though the sea breeze kept it from being completely merciless. What were summers in Ohio like? She couldn't imagine living anywhere but here. Though she'd been born and raised in Pennsylvania until she was ten, she considered Wildwood home in every sense of the word, had loved it as soon as she set eyes on it. There was something magical about living in a place that so many people traveled to for an escape, of knowing a place inside and out in a way the tourists never would.

And of course there were benefits to having so much family here. Her parents still lived in the gray house on Cedar Street where they'd raised their twelve children, and though a few of those children had moved away like Win, Florie liked to joke that there were nearly as many Carlisles in Wildwood as there were seashells. She couldn't think how she would have managed to get by these past few years if she hadn't had her mother, sisters and nieces to help her look after the boys.

This summer her sixteen-year-old niece Dolly had all but

moved in with her, managing the house and the boys with wonderful efficiency. Come September there would be less to arrange, with all three boys attending school. Dolly or Dolly's younger sister, Mary, could collect them each afternoon and stay with them until Florie got home. Perhaps by next year she could trust Billy with that task; he was a good, sensible boy, and he'd be ten by then, old enough to take a few hours' responsibility.

If they were here, of course. In Ohio she supposed she'd be home to greet them every day.

She went up the path to their little house, the only thing of value Bill had left her with. The boys exploded from the door, a mob of towheads and wild limbs, frenetic in their rush to get to her. Their voices blurred together as they recounted the days' events, and she nodded agreeably, not caring that she caught one word in every ten, until she heard, "Uncle Jim."

"What?" she asked, convinced she'd misheard. Her sisters were marrying at a furious pace this past year, and she did a silent run-through of their husbands' names, certain one of them must sound like—

"Uncle Jim," Billy repeated. "You remember him, don't you?"

She nearly laughed, because she'd known Jim since she was a child. "I didn't think *you'd* remember him," she said. "It's been a couple years."

"I'm not a baby," Billy said scornfully. "Harry didn't know him, but I did."

"I did so know him!" Harry protested. He was only a year younger than Billy, and hated when he was treated in any way inferior. "It just took me a minute."

"I knew him straight off," Billy said smugly.

Florie's mind was awhirl, but she steered the boys towards the house before saying, "And what did Uncle Jim want?"

"He came to see you," Harry said, at the same time Carl piped up with, "He gave us Turkish taffy."

"He said he'd come back this evening," Billy added. "Dolly told him you'd be in then. Can I stay up?"

"We'll see," Florie said absently. "Get yourselves washed up for supper. Did you set the table yet?"

The boys scurried off, and Florie stuck her head into the kitchen, where Dolly was slicing tomatoes. She looked up as Florie came in. "You heard we had a visitor?"

"The boys told me."

"I tried to invite him for supper, but he wouldn't accept. Said he'd come by after."

Florie nodded, trying to think what to say.

"He looked same as always," Dolly went on, shooting her a mischievous grin. "Right fine."

"Never mind that," Florie said and went to change out of her work clothes. She hesitated a moment, nearly putting on her good church dress, but Dolly would be sure to notice—and comment. She put on her usual skirt and blouse, shaking her head. When had she ever dressed up for Jim?

Supper seemed extremely long. Afterwards she had Dolly

take the boys down to the beach while she cleaned up. They were more than happy to go; Dolly could visit her friends, and the boys could get rid of the last of their energy before bed.

After washing the dishes, Florie settled down on the sofa with the newspaper, trying to act like she wasn't peeking out the window every few seconds.

When Jim finally appeared, Florie nearly sat back and pretended she hadn't been waiting, but what was the point of silly games? It was just Jim; why shouldn't she be eager to see him? She opened the door before he could knock and watched his face break into a grin she could already feel herself returning.

She invited him in, gave him a quick hug. He looked just the same—a little thinner, perhaps, but that was all. "It's good to see you," she said. "Come into the kitchen, and I'll make tea."

"You don't have to bother over me," he said, but she was already halfway to the stove, glad to have something to busy herself with.

"Have you been back long?" she asked, putting the kettle on and cutting him a slice of apple cake. He'd joined the Navy a week after America declared war; they'd exchanged a few letters, but their correspondence had gradually petered off.

Jim shook his head. "Stayed with a friend in Philadelphia for a bit, but Wildwood's in my blood."

"Where are you living?" She knew his widowed mother had remarried and moved out west last year, and he didn't have any other family.

Except her boys, of course. Jim and Bill had been cousins.

"Got myself a boat, and I'm sleeping on that. It's not as big as the *Florabelle*, but I can make decent money fishing till the weather turns, and then I'll see about winter."

She nodded, turning back to the tea preparations. Hearing the name of his and Bill's old boat, sold to cover some of the debts, still stung. Jim had been Bill's business partner, taking tourists out fishing.

"The boys sure have grown," Jim said as she brought him the tea.

"They do tend to do that." She'd meant to make him laugh, but he just toyed with the handle of his teacup.

"Billy told me about Bill," he said, still looking down. "My condolences."

She tried to find a proper response and settled for, "Either way he was never coming back, was he?" She took a sip of her own tea, which tasted of tears. "The idiotic man. I'm sure he never volunteered, which meant he was drafted. And he could have exempted himself if he said he was the breadwinner of a household with small children. But no. He'd rather go to war than come back to us." She plunked the teacup down with more force than she meant to, splattering the tablecloth. "I wasn't even listed as his next of kin. Had to hear about his death secondhand from his mother." She'd sounded ashamed in her letter, as though she couldn't believe her treasured son had managed to turn out so bad.

"Enough of that," Florie said, because Jim was still

frowning down at his tea like he was wishing he could be anywhere else. "Would you like the family rundown?"

"Of course," he said, and she went through the Carlisle news of the past few years, all the weddings and babies and whatnot. Jim had been her first friend when she'd arrived in Wildwood as a child, and sometimes she thought he'd befriended her just because he'd been fascinated by her enormous family.

So she entertained him with all the family shenanigans until he was done with his tea and cake. "I'd better be going," he said.

"I'd try to talk you into staying, but if you're here when the boys get back, I'll never get them to bed. But you must come to supper tomorrow."

"I don't want to impose..."

"Nonsense. You're family," she said briskly, and he finally agreed to come.

Supper the next evening was as loud as Florie could remember it being, with the boys peppering Jim with all sorts of questions about everything from the war to fishing. He agreed to take them out on the boat the next day, and though Carl got seasick, Billy and Harry enjoyed themselves so much that Jim proposed taking them every day. Florie tried to protest that he surely didn't need to, but Jim insisted, and it made Dolly's day easier, so she finally agreed.

Days took on a new rhythm after that, with Billy and Harry

coming home each day bubbling with stories and pride. "Best crew I ever had," Jim boasted, and the two boys puffed up like bullfrogs. Florie knew they must be more trouble than help, but she didn't dare voice this in front of them, and when she did to Jim alone, he waved her words away.

"They're fine boys."

"Yes, but—"

"You leave them to me. We get on all right."

They kept her supplied with fresh fish, and Florie managed to convince Jim to stay to supper most nights. She'd fry up the fish, and afterwards they'd go down to the beach or the boardwalk, where Jim would buy the boys ice cream or taffy, and sometimes rides on the new merry-go-round, which seemed a terrible extravagance.

"You'll spoil them," she said, watching as the boys picked their garish horses with glee.

"They're not milk, Florie. Your boys are hard to spoil. And Billy and Harry work hard for me all day." He paused. "Shall we join them?"

She laughed and let him drag her over, and she picked the brightest, silliest looking horse of them all. Somehow when Jim was around she felt like a girl again, not a thirty-one-year-old widow.

Florie's older sister Mabel came to visit the last week of August with her husband and babies. They stayed with Mother and Father, but they came to supper at Florie's on their third night there.

Afterwards Florie and Mabel did the washing up together. Jim and Mabel's husband Fred were outside with the children, and it was easy to imagine she and Florie were young again, two schoolgirls gossiping in the kitchen. "Do you miss it here?" Florie asked. Mabel lived in northern New Jersey, away from the ocean.

"Goodness knows there's nowhere else like it," Mabel said, "but no, I don't particularly miss it. Not everyone's meant to live in fairyland."

Florie looked at her in surprise; it was a fanciful thing to say, and Mabel wasn't normally a fanciful person.

Of course Florie didn't consider herself a particularly fanciful person, either. A woman with three boys to raise and no husband couldn't afford to be fanciful. Perhaps she wasn't meant to live in fairyland, either.

"I see Jim Chavery's hanging around," Mabel said, drying the last of the plates.

"You make him sound like a stray dog," Florie protested.

Mabel raised her eyebrows. "I always thought he was a bit like a dog. So loyal to you. So devoted." Her tone dripped with disdain.

"Don't," Florie said quietly. She'd forgotten how opinionated Mabel could be, to the point of rudeness.

"You must see it. It's not right to lead him on, Florie. People will talk."

"The way they talked when Bill left?" She heard her voice rising, but couldn't seem to reign it in. "I do hope, wherever he was before he died, that he got talked about, too. Because surely he was the one who deserved it."

But of course he wouldn't have been talked about. That was the point of leaving, wasn't it? You could start over, and no one knew anything about you, about your history, about your mistakes.

"Now, now," Mabel clucked. "No use getting riled over things you can't change."

Florie felt well and truly riled, and her sister's words just added to her irritation.

Mabel stowed the plates in the cupboard. "Has Winfield written to you yet?"

"Hmmm?" Florie grunted, still angry.

"I told him he should invite you out. Give you a fresh start away from here."

Florie nearly dropped the cup she was drying. "*You* told Win to ask me to move out there?"

Mabel smiled, cat-like and satisfied. "Of course. It would be good for both of you."

So Win wasn't terribly lonely and wanting her company. He was just giving in to Mabel's meddling in a way that Florie had never been inclined to do.

She set the cup down and left the room, mumbling something about a headache and a need for rest. Mabel could be infuriating, but there was no use bickering with her. In the quiet of her bedroom she finally wrote the letter to Win, thanking him for his offer, but explaining she couldn't possibly accept. Her life was here, and she wasn't leaving.

Florie didn't see Jim until the following evening. He'd asked mid-week if he could take her out to supper on Saturday, and she'd agreed readily enough then. Now, with Mabel's words echoing in her head, she wished she hadn't, but she could hardly cancel.

She put on her newest dress—not fancy, but at least fresh—and her good hat. When Jim arrived, looking all spruced up in a blue summer suit, she kissed the boys goodnight and reminded them to listen to Dolly, then let Jim take her by the arm and lead her through the bustling streets to the lights of fairyland.

"Nowhere fancy," she said firmly, so they had hamburgers in a little place that overlooked the ocean. She relaxed, because she wasn't going to let Mabel ruin her evening. Jim was just Jim, always good company.

When Bill had been courting her he'd always chattered on at meals in a way Florie had found endearing because she could hear the nervousness beneath his words and knew he wanted to impress her. But this wasn't a date, and she and Jim had known each other too long to ever be nervous in each other's company. They talked about all sorts of things—family, the war, books—their words flowing as easily as they did over the supper table at home.

Afterwards they strolled the boardwalk. Jim bought ice cream cones, and Florie thoroughly enjoyed hers, so delicious and cold. It was nearly dark now, and the lights of the boardwalk twinkled like stars. She felt like she was seeing it for the first time, now that she knew she wasn't leaving.

"Do you want to go dancing?" Jim asked.

Noise spilled from the dance hall on the pier, chatter overlapping the music, raucous laughter. Florie could remember Bill taking her dancing, her flushed excitement always ending with sore feet, an aching head and an embarrassing amount of perspiration. "Not here," she said, and laughed at Jim's puzzlement as she took him by the hand and led him off the boardwalk.

Down on the beach, the lights were muted and the music had a muffled, ethereal quality, as though they'd actually stumbled into fairyland. Florie kicked off her shoes and peeled off her stockings, wriggling her toes against the sand as Jim did likewise.

"Can I have this dance?" Jim asked, and she relaxed against him. They were one with the night, the beach, the twinkling magic of Wildwood.

"I got a letter from my mate in Philadelphia," Jim said. "He's got himself a job at the rail station, thinks he can get me hired on, too."

"You're leaving?"

"Not for another couple months yet. But I can hardly live on the boat come winter, and it doesn't seem worth staying here unless..." She felt the rise of his chest as he drew a deep breath. "Unless I had a reason to stay."

She looked at him, waiting for him to go on. He didn't.

"A reason like me?" she prompted.

He nodded. "I'd do my best to provide for you and the boys. You know I love them like my own. And you. I've loved you since I was ten years old, Florie."

His words washed against her, all but bowling her over. She buried her face in Jim's chest, and to her humiliation she found herself crying, the tears soaking into the front of his shirt. What was wrong with her? She rarely cried, and never publicly like this, never—

They were still swaying to the music, slow and hypnotic, and she did her best to snuffle away the tears, though she knew Jim must realize she was crying.

"Sorry," she said once she'd gotten hold of herself again. She broke away from him and fished in her pocket for a handkerchief. "I got your shirt all wet."

He laughed softly. "I work on a boat, Florie. I'm used to wet."

"The last time I cried like that was when I heard Bill died. I don't know why I cried for him."

"He was your husband."

She snorted. "Hardly, at that point. I think it was more that it was the end. That I'd never get to find out why he left. Never get to give him what for."

"That makes sense. I used to have whole conversations with him in my head, right after he left. Asking him how he could ever do such a thing to you. I never could imagine a good answer."

"Because there wasn't one."

"I suppose not. I wanted there to be, though. Because

otherwise my cousin was just a rotten human being, and what did that say about me that I never noticed?"

She felt her breath catch, that someone else felt that way. "I was married to him and didn't suspect a thing was wrong. He shattered my whole life when he left—not just the money, the security, but me. That trust I had in myself, that I could know a terrible person if I saw one." She looked at him. "That's why I don't want to ask you to stay."

"Because you think I'm like Bill?"

He sounded horrified, and why shouldn't he? Of course he wasn't Bill, would never be Bill. Surely she knew that.

"I understand if you don't have feelings for me, but don't think I would ever, ever do anything like that to you, Florie."

She nodded hard, because she knew that, she'd always known that even as she'd doubted herself. Every bit of magic from her childhood, every sparkling memory, included Jim. She'd loved him since she was ten years old, too—not in any romantic way, not then, but in the purest, safest way love could be.

A way she'd never felt with Bill, for all he'd made her swoon. Oh, she'd felt secure in her life with him until it had all fallen apart, but she'd never known every single part of him, the way she knew Jim. She hadn't realized it then, but she knew it was true.

"I know that," she said, putting all the certainty she could into the words. "I do."

"Good."

She wanted to explain to him everything that was dawning

on her, everything she should have realized sooner. But instead she said quietly, "Do you remember that summer we were convinced there was a creature living in the woods?"

"It came out of the ocean and lost its gills," Jim said like he was recounting something completely factual. "And it wandered amongst the trees at night moaning and wailing because it wanted to get back to the sea."

"We snuck away one evening to try to catch it, and I was so scared, but I held your hand and pretended I wasn't." She wove her fingers through his now, delighting in how familiar it felt. "I was eleven years old, and I thought I was all grown up."

"I was scared, too," he said.

"I remember," she said. "But we were brave together. We trusted each other." She took a deep breath of salt air. "That's what love is, isn't it? Trusting in someone else, even when it's terrifying."

He looked at her, and she could see the hope welling in his eyes.

"I want you to stay," she said. "For the winter. Forever. With me and the boys. Would you do that?"

"Of course."

"I love you," she said, and leaned in to kiss him, not caring in the least who might be watching, who might gossip about it later. Let them talk. She knew exactly what she was doing, and it felt marvelous.

A Race to Finish
MELANIE MULROONEY

Johanna Collins surveyed the ballroom, barely able to contain her excitement—built as it was over ten long weeks of anticipation. Dozens of pink peonies and red roses sat in elegant arrangements, filling the room with a heady perfume. The very best of society was in attendance wearing their finest attire in a riot of colours, and the air was buzzing with their whispers of admiration and assessment. Everything was perfection.

"The Walkertons have surely exceeded expectations." Mrs Collins rubbed at imaginary blemishes on Johanna's pristine gown, which was made from an embroidered green silk and fit her exquisitely.

"To think, a future son-in-law—or two—could be in our midst this evening." Glee at the mere prospect lit her mother's face. "I should be very relieved to see both my girls settled."

Johanna gently brushed her mother's hand aside, giving

it a light squeeze of affection. Newly two and twenty, she was certainly ready to marry and establish her own home, and she knew the same to be true for her sister, Anne. If their plan went well this evening, perhaps one of them would confirm their match.

"Mrs Collins. How lovely to see you." Johanna turned to find William Croft—her brother's oldest friend, and her childhood torment—engaging her mother in conversation. Now a man full grown, his features had resolved into handsome lines, his physical movements more deliberate, no longer those of a gangly boy. He turned towards her, and Johanna noted that his eyes still possessed a joyful spark— one she remembered as a distinct sign of trouble.

"Mr Croft." Johanna dipped a slight curtsey and offered her hand. "I had not heard you were in town."

"Miss Collins." Croft enveloped her gloved hand in both of his. "It was time I returned. I have business to tend to and promises to keep." His eyes twinkled with merriment, holding her gaze a beat longer than necessary before breaking away to look about the group. "And where is Miss Anne this evening? Do not tell me you are no longer joined at the hip with your younger sister?"

"Anne is at home abed, covered in hives after an unfortunate encounter with a bee earlier this afternoon," Johanna said, ignoring the censuring look from her mother. Surely there was no need for that level of propriety with William Croft, who was more family to them all than a respectable gentleman of mere acquaintance. "She was horribly disappointed to miss the ball and has extracted my promise to relay every excruciating detail."

"Ah. Well, you shall need to exert yourself as fully as possible to bring back a tale worth telling." Something about the way he said the words *exert yourself* seemed to reach through Johanna and tug at her insides. She quickly brushed the thought aside.

"I declare I am up to the task."

William cocked a brow at this. "And what details have you noted for Anne so far, might I ask?"

"Well, she will doubtless want to hear of droll Mr Fitzwilliam, standing near the card room with a sour expression, offering complaints with the pretense that he was merely joking." William let out a bark of laughter. "And I shan't forget to tell her about Mr Elliot, whose eye constantly roams the room, assessing the young ladies like one might appraise a fattened hog at market."

William's smile was dazzling. "And is there no man in attendance worthy of your good opinion, Jo?"

Her gaze settled on Mr Barnaby Smythe. His looks were amiable, manners mild. He sported a canary yellow waistcoat with an ornate design more intricate than any gown in the room, topped by a wool coat in the deepest shade of crimson. She was as yet undecided, but planned to know soon enough if his character was one of fashion or fortune.

"That remains to be seen."

William followed her gaze. "Indeed."

Mrs Collins broke through the private moment, regaining

William's attention and inquiring after his family back home in Scotland. After a minute of polite nodding, Johanna shifted her attention back to Barnaby, who was now in conversation with the extremely pretty—and eternally insipid—Kitty Brown. Kitty fluttered her fan invitingly beneath dark-lashed eyes as Barnaby engaged her with banter that Johanna was unable to hear from across the room. He extended a hand, and Kitty—simpering as always—lowered her fan and allowed him to lead her out to dance.

"Would you care to dance, Jo?" Croft's voice was little more than a whisper and seemed entirely too close for comfort.

Johanna's head shot around. "With you?"

He released a low, throaty laugh. "I'm sure you could have your pick of the room, but yes, I am extending my hand. If you are not otherwise engaged?" A blush rose high in Johanna's cheeks as she mumbled her acquiescence and placed her hand in his once again.

The couple moved through the sea of silk and muslin and wool and faced each other in line with the other dancers waiting for the Sussex Waltz to begin.

Johanna stood in silence, unable to think of what to say. This was the boy that delighted in pulling her hair and leaving spiders in her shoes. Now here he was, a man grown, and they were dealing with new and unusual circumstances. He seemed a stranger in this moment, though she felt she could not treat him as such, talking as if they were mere acquaintances. Nor could she speak candidly as if he were still the young boy of her youth. She found the situation decidedly confusing.

If he were a true gentleman, he would lead the conversation and put her out of her misery. But he just stood there, staring at her like he would memorize her every feature. She had the urge to run straight from the room.

"Have you been—"

"How was your—"

A smile spread across William's handsome face, and Johanna could not help but return it.

"After you, Jo."

"Oh. I was going to inquire about your journey from Scotland. How was the weather during your travels? It has been quite wet here this season and exceedingly muddy." She had decided to treat him like a stranger after all. And now she was rambling and making the worst type of awkward conversation, which topped her list of most hated activities.

The pianoforte started at last, and William stepped toward her, hand outstretched. "The weather was lovely, thank you," he whispered as they passed each other, arms entwined. "I am sorry for the muddy season and hope your skirt hems have survived." His eyes shone.

Johanna recalled a time when he took great pleasure in the ruin of her skirt hems. He would claim that she could not possibly race him to this tree or that, knowing she would never turn down a dare. And then he would sprint off on the most unkempt path available, letting her trail through muck and mud after him. She could never quite keep up, but somehow, she always managed to overtake him so that their races ended neck-in-neck in the end. Before this moment, she had not considered that he had allowed her to catch him.

"My hems fare much better these days, thank you. I suppose the many scoldings from my governess finally helped me change my ways." She danced past him again, heard his soft chuckle, and felt the heat from his body as it brushed past hers.

She recalled the last time they raced each other. Judging by the piercing look William gave her now, she would bet her pin money that he was remembering that same day.

They had all been on the cusp of leaving their childhood, and it was the last season William had spent at his family's country home. The mid-summer heat was thick in the air as Johanna and William raced off toward the lake, leaving their siblings behind. They took respite from the sun in the lakeside gazebo, waiting for the others to catch up. William had tucked a loose strand of hair behind her ear and looked at her in a way that felt vastly different from any look she had received prior. She had thought about those sweet moments and the words that followed many times since.

She raised a finger to her lips, and heat rose to her cheeks at the memory. Good heavens, was she to spend the entire ball blushing for this man?

Johanna shook her head, reminding herself of her purpose this evening. She looked about at the other dancers, the majority of whom were single young people looking for a match. To her surprise, Barnaby and Kitty no longer seemed to be among them.

"Are you searching for someone in particular, Jo?" William stepped past Johanna in time with the music, his footwork light and sure, the intricate steps causing him no trouble.

"Oh. No. Just admiring the room." Heat still burned in Johanna's cheeks.

At last, the music paused. She thought she saw Barnaby's crimson coattails by the refreshments table.

"I am feeling a little parched. Perhaps it is time for a glass of lemonade."

"Please allow me to escort you." William extended an arm and led her from the dance floor.

Johanna held the small glass of lemonade, running one gloved finger around the rim. She found her focus split between chatting amiably with William and keeping an eye on Barnaby, now seated in conversation with Kitty across the room. She could only overhear an occasional word or moment of laughter. Certainly not enough to ascertain if they were engaged in a serious flirtation.

"I daresay you'd agree?" William cocked his head, eyebrow raised.

"Oh. Yes, of course."

He let out a bark of laughter. "My, how times have changed, Jo. I never thought I'd hear you admit that women are not as suited to sport as men."

Johanna stared at him in horror. They had argued this point for years. "What? Indeed I never—" She ran a hand across her brow, releasing a sigh. She might as well own to it. "You've caught me out, William. I apologize for my wandering attention."

William's smile turned from amusement to kindness. "No matter, Jo. I was merely teasing. Is everything well? Is there anything I can do to assist you?" He reached out a hand and touched the bare skin of her arm. She stared at his fingers which seemed to linger for an eternity. The heat from his contact—the familiarity—was nearly unbearable. She would not be caught up again in yearning for this man.

Johanna tore her eyes away and forced herself to look at his face. "No William, it's quite alright." The moment was broken by a glimpse of crimson wool passing through the balcony door. "Though I do think I need a moment of air. If you'll excuse me." Johanna hastened out the door in pursuit.

The patio provided a clear view of the large and well-manicured gardens. The warm breeze carried the scent of Lady Walkerton's beloved lilacs, currently in peak bloom. Johanna took a moment to orient herself, searching for signs of Barnaby and Kitty. Surely they would not be foolish enough to head out of sight, putting Kitty in a position that could ruin her were she discovered? Was Barnaby Smythe that sort of man? Even Kitty Brown deserved better treatment than this.

Johanna headed towards the hedge in search of the wayward couple. She was mere steps inside the shadows when she felt a hand on her shoulder. She turned to find William staring down at her, looking decidedly agitated.

"Johanna. What are you up to?"

"William! I am…looking for someone."

"Looking for someone? Who could you possibly be looking for out here, alone, in the gardens?"

This time, the heat rising in Johanna's cheeks was fueled by anger. Truth be told, she did not know exactly why she was out here, risking her reputation to spy on Barnaby Smythe. But she would not answer to William Croft. "That is hardly any of your business, sir."

"None of my business?" William's brows shot up.

"Perhaps I should ask what *you* are doing out here alone in the gardens? Are you spying on me, William?"

"Never mind me, Jo." William took a step closer to her, his eyes flashing an emotion she did not recognize. "Tell me you are not here for a rendezvous."

"Good heavens. I am not *meeting* anyone. I merely followed Barnaby, as I thought he might be meeting with Kitty."

"Barnaby Smythe?" William's hands flexed at his sides. "Jo, he is not good enough for you. He's a spendthrift and a rake and drowning in gambling debts." He stepped towards her, gripping her by the shoulders. "You cannot marry a man such as that, Jo."

"Me? Marry Barnaby Smythe?" Johanna snorted an indelicate laugh. "I would rather run away to the Americas."

William looked confused. "If you do not care to marry the man, why on earth have you spent the evening spying upon him?" William's hands softened on her shoulders, shifting down to cup her bare upper arms. "Johanna, what is going on?"

She shivered under his touch. "It's Anne. Barnaby has been paying her particular attention with hints of a betrothal to come. She charged me with watching him this evening to report back on his behaviour in her absence. I am merely attempting to assess his character and suitability as a future brother."

Relief washed over William's face, and he took another step toward her. Johanna realized just how close he was standing, his body mere inches from hers. He murmured, "So you have no interest in him for yourself?"

"No," she breathed.

His hands moved gently up her arms. "Will Anne be horribly disappointed?"

"She shall be devastated, which will suit her well. She has always loved the chase more than the capture."

"And what about you, Jo? Do you wish to be caught?" He wrapped a finger in a loose curl and tugged gently. He had done this a thousand times, annoying her to no end. But this time, she did not feel annoyed; the tug shot straight to her insides, causing a riot of sensations deep in her belly.

"I...William..." She felt unmoored. What was he saying?

"Do you remember the day at the lake, Jo?" His lips were inches from hers now just as they had been then. "Do you remember my promise?"

"You shall have to remind me, William." Her heart thundered in her chest. Had he thought about that moment all these years, waiting for her, as she did him?

"I promised that if you were not married by two and twenty, I would be back to make you mine."

"Oh, yes. That promise." She stared up into his eyes, searching.

"Was it not your birthday last month, Jo?"

"Yes, William, it was." She spread her hand against his chest, feeling his heartbeat racing to meet hers.

"So perhaps you'd agree it's time we made good on that vow." He ran a finger along her cheek.

Johanna leaned her face into his hand, reveling in the feel of his touch. "Just one thing first, William." She looked past his shoulder to the edge of the rose garden. "You'll have to race me to that hawthorn tree." And she was off with a whoop of joy, the sound of his laughter close on her heels.

As she reached the tree she felt his strong arms wrap around her waist. She turned to look up into William's beaming face and saw triumph, love, and something new and utterly exciting.

"We've reached the finish line, Jo. I'm here to claim my prize." His lips met hers and she melted into his embrace.

Perhaps this time they'd both take the win. After all, she did let him catch her.

Tangled Web
MAUREEN BOWDEN

This annual ritual made my stomach churn. The employees of Hopkins, Hopkins and Platt, Chartered Accountants, were sitting around in the office canteen discussing summer holidays.

Tim Platt was considering Malta, Angela Daley was trying to talk Freddie Banks into accompanying her to the Dominican Republic, and Sophie Melancamp had already booked a flight to Magaluf. I concentrated on my cheese and piccalilli sandwiches and hoped they'd ignore me. No such luck.

Freddie asked, "Where are you going, Emily?"

I said the first thing that came into my head. "Italy. I've always wanted to explore the ruins of Pompeii."

The truth was I was terrified of flying but too embarrassed to admit that I wouldn't be going anywhere further than a guest house in Skegness, twenty-six miles from my home town of Louth.

I had to tell my mother that I'd lied. She and her 'friend,' (to use a euphemism) Peter, were acquainted with two of my bosses, Jack and Jessica Hopkins, and I didn't want her to accidentally give me away. She said, "Why didn't you tell the truth, Emily? They'd understand after what happened to your father."

I sulked. "That lot wouldn't. They think anyone who doesn't fly off to somewhere hot and trendy every year is a freak."

That night my father's ghost scolded me. "What a tangled web we weave."

"It was only a white lie, Dad, and anyway, it's your fault. If you hadn't nose-dived into the Indian Ocean in 2004 I wouldn't have a flying phobia."

"To be fair, Emily, it was the pilot who nose-dived. The passengers couldn't do a helluva lot about it."

I knew I shouldn't be angry with him for charging off to Thailand on a mercy mission to help the survivors of the tsunami, but I needed him too.

My living, breathing dad was now just a fuzzy memory of a big man holding me in his arms when I was no more than three years old. He was singing a pop song about everybody changing and not knowing why. Then everything changed, and I didn't know why. The only father I'd had for the last seventeen years was his ghost.

Holiday time arrived, and I checked into 'Cobblestone Corner' guest house, Skegness. The ghost came with me.

The sea and the sun were satisfactory and the nightclubs

even better. I hooked up with a group of art students celebrating their graduation. They were fun, especially Max: untidy ginger curls scraped back into a top-knot, and a smile to die for. I was well pleased to discover that he was also from Louth. We lived within jogging distance of each other. Who needs Pompeii?

"What do you think of him?" I asked the ghost.

"He's rather too pleased with himself. They all are at that age."

"Were you?"

"Definitely not. I was modest, self-effacing and frequently carried old ladies' shopping."

"Liar."

"It takes one to know one."

The Friday evening before I returned home Max and I sat together on the shore. An elderly couple were strolling along the sand with their pet dog that was splashing and scampering in the North Sea breakers. They looked content. That could have been my parents' future. Why didn't Mum marry again? I hated to think of her growing old alone.

I borrowed the pencil Max always carried, and pulled out of my bag the envelope that had contained my guest house reservation. On the back of it I sketched his face and signed it, Emily Hollis.

"Something to remember me by," I said.

He took it. "You're good, Emz. Better than me. Did you ever think of studying art?"

"Not really. I needed a job to help Mum, so I ended up as

a trainee accountant."

He tucked the drawing into his pocket. "I'm hoping to start my own business designing and making jewellery. You're wasted in accountancy. If you ever want a career change let me know." We exchanged addresses and phone numbers. "I'll make you a pair of earrings as a thank you for the portrait. I'm designing a collection based on the zodiac. What's your birth sign?"

"Pisces. Am I going to have fishes dangling from my ears?"

"Wait and see."

Next morning I caught the National Express bus home, unaware that while I'd been clubbing in Skeggy, Mount Vesuvius had erupted.

My mother was unpacking a shopping bag in the kitchen. A posy of lilies and carnations sat on the breakfast bar.

"Who are the flowers for?" I asked "Is somebody dead?"

"You, according to the staff of Hopkins, Hopkins and Platt. I don't suppose you've heard the news about Vesuvius. Pompeii's covered in lava again." She picked up the sympathy card that accompanied the flowers and skimmed it towards me like a paper aeroplane. "The tourists had nowhere to run. There were no survivors."

My head spun. I sat down before my legs buckled and I stared at her, speechless. She shoved an economy sized packet of cornflakes into the food cupboard and turned to face me. "Close your mouth, Emily. You look like a fish."

I tried to stop my voice from trembling. "How many were killed?"

"Nobody knows yet. The mountain's still rumbling. It's too dangerous for anyone to take a look. When they do, your workmates might ask for the flowers back, so I hope they last."

I ignored the sarcasm. "Why didn't you tell them I wasn't there?"

"Because I didn't know what fib you'd come up with to explain why you weren't. You'd better get over there on Monday morning before they give your job to someone else. How was Skeggy?"

"Very nice, thank you."

The ghost was no more sympathetic. He sat on the edge of my bed that night. "The white lie dropped you in a load of fertilizer, girl. What's the escape plan?"

"There isn't one. Do you have any suggestions?"

"Yes, tell the truth."

"Not helpful."

Monday morning dawned, and I had my story ready. The open-plan office fell silent when I walked in. I approached Jessica's desk, and the next white lie tumbled out while it was still fresh in my mind.

"I didn't go. On the morning of my flight I woke up with a stonking headache, feeling sick and shivering all over. It was a flu bug. After a few days I felt better but a bit fragile, so I went to Skeggy to recuperate. It was very nice. Thank you for the flowers."

Everyone started talking at once, and Sophie Melancamp nearly suffocated me in a bear-hug. "I'm so glad you're not dead, Emz. Luv you to bits. Come to Magaluf with me next year." I'd need a whopper of a white lie to avert that one.

Jessica and Jack glanced at each other, frowning. Jessica said, "We're obviously very relieved that you're okay, Emily, but I'm afraid we have bad news. You know how busy we are. We had to replace you, and our nephew, George, has recently completed his Association of Accounting Technicians Course, so we gave him your job."

For the first time I noticed the pale, skinny, young man sitting at my desk. He blushed and half-waved his arm to me. I half-waved back.

Jack said, "We'll give you a glowing reference. You should have no trouble finding another job. We'll send you your holiday pay to tide you over, and you're welcome to keep the flowers."

I said my goodbyes and fled. I'd barely passed through the swing doors when Sophie caught up with me.

She grabbed my arm. "You can't let them get away with this, Emz. It isn't right."

I shook my head. "Leave it, Sophe. They haven't done anything wrong."

"Neither have you. This is unfair, but don't you worry. I'm going to fix it. See ya later."

She ran back inside, and I silently groaned. Sophie loves a crusade. Her pit-bull interlocking jaws take hold when she finds one, and she doesn't let go.

Mum was working as a classroom assistant at the local primary school that couldn't afford enough teachers. She rang me in her lunch break to find out what happened. I told her the tale.

"I won't say it's your own fault, Emily, although it is, but I do think they've been a bit quick off the mark in replacing you."

I took a deep breath. "There's worse, Mum. Sophie Melancamp's rampaging through Louth with her flaming sword again, howling for vengeance."

"Yes, she would. Boudicca in Lycra leggings. Never mind her. Get on the government website, make a claim for Job Seekers Allowance and start seeking."

Four hours later I was immersed in the impenetrable maze of the Internet when the doorbell rang. Sophie stood on the step alongside a sharp-eyed woman, thirty-ish, carrying a notebook with an attached pen. A complicated looking camera was slung over her shoulder.

She held out her free hand and flashed her dental implants at me. "Miss Hollis? I'm Julie Gahooley, head reporter for The Daily Oracle. May I call you Emily?"

I knew her name. The local newspaper, commonly known as the Orifice, had only one reporter and loan paparazza. Julie Gahooly never let truth, overwhelming evidence or the laws of physics get in the way of a good story. She left out the boring bits and filled the gaps with her own lurid imagination.

"May we come in?" She swept past me, into the living room, with Sophie in her wake. The ghost was sitting crossed-legged on the coffee table. He raised his eyes and shrugged.

I'd had enough of this. "Before either of you speak," I said, "I have something to say." Julie opened the notebook and sat in Mum's favourite armchair with her pen poised. Sophie perched on the arm of the couch, ready to spring into action. I told them about my father's death, my flying phobia and my cowardly white lies. Neither of them noticed my mother come in and stand in the doorway, listening.

Julie looked up from her scribbling. "Great. I can see the headline, 'Local hero's daughter, victim of unfair dismissal.' We'll not only get you your job back, Emily, we'll get a memorial to your father in the town square, with a statue of him pulling a child out of the encroaching ocean."

Sophie punched the air. "Whoo hoo. Count me in."

"But he never even got to Thailand," I said.

My mother stepped into the room. "This stops now," she said. "It's all lies, but not Emily's. They're mine." She turned to me. "I'm sorry, sweetheart. Your father isn't dead. He was never on a mercy mission to Thailand, he ran off with a chiropodist from Torquay. I believed it would be kinder to let you believe he was a hero rather than—"

"A love-rat," I interrupted.

"Yes. I may have been wrong but I meant well."

She looked so lost and vulnerable; I flung my arms around her. "It's okay, Mum. I know you did."

"Aren't you angry with me?"

"I'll probably be livid when all this sinks in, but right now I'm curious. Are you actually divorced?"

"Oh, yes, years ago."

"So why didn't you marry Peter?"

"I thought you'd hate me for being unfaithful to your father's memory."

"If I'd known the truth I wouldn't."

Julie stopped scribbling and looked up from her notebook. "Great. I've got it. 'Abandoned child of love-rat father, sacked because she's afraid to fly.' What do you think, Emily?"

I glared at her. "It's a lie."

"Well, technically speaking, yes, but there is a connection. Call it lateral thinking."

Mum spoke quietly but with coldness I'd never seen in her before. "We won't call it anything. If you print one sentence about my family I'll have words with your editor, Bob Wragg. His cousin, Peter is a close friend of mine and he knows things that Bob wouldn't want made public. Do we understand each other?"

Julie closed her notebook.

"Of course, Mrs Hollis, the boys all have their secrets. We'd best not go there." She gave us what she apparently considered a conspiratorial wink, and turned to Sophie. "Let's go, Sophe. There's no story here. I'm sure your friend will soon find another job that doesn't involve flying."

For once, Sophie was Che Guevara without a revolution.

I escorted them to the door. Before they left Julie said, "By the way, Emily, I noticed you have a ghost. Trust me, you can't believe anything they say."

How true. I'd deal with him later, but there was another

matter I needed to discuss with my mother first. She was in the kitchen making coffee. Her hand was shaking.

"Sit down before you scald yourself," I said. "I'll do that."

She nodded and sat at the breakfast bar. I made hers as she likes it, with exactly one and a half spoonfuls of sugar. I carried over our cups and sat beside her. "Have you been swindling the Department of Works and Pensions?" I said.

"No. What are you talking about?"

"The widow's pension that you told me is paid into your bank account every month."

"Another white lie, I'm afraid. That's maintenance for you from your father." She sipped her coffee. "While you were at school I needed it but since you started work I've been paying it into a separate bank account for you. There's a nice little nest egg waiting whenever you need it."

"So he does care a little bit about me."

"He cares a lot about you. He asked me to write to him at least four times a year telling him how you are and what you're doing."

"Tell him I want to meet him."

She grasped my hand. "I will, I promise, and I'm so sorry I deceived you. Once I told the first lie I thought there was no going back. I'll write to him tonight."

She was still trembling. "You're in no fit state tonight. Tomorrow will be soon enough. Is he still with the chiropodist?"

"No idea. I never ask."

I drank my coffee in silence.

She said, "Are you okay, Emily?"

"Yes, but would you mind if I went to my room for a little while? There's a lot I need to get my head round."

"Of course there is. Take as long as you want. I'll wash up."

The ghost sat on my windowsill looking sheepish. I always spoke to him in whispers so Mum wouldn't hear, but I tried to make this whisper a fierce one. "Spill. Who or what the hell are you?"

He smiled my father's smile. "I'm a pain parasite."

"Never heard of them. Expand."

"There are millions of us. We latch onto folk suffering the pain of loss, become what they want us to be and tell them whatever will bring them comfort. As their pain leaves them we feed on it. It's a symbiotic relationship."

"You lie to them."

"We tell them what they need to hear. They're white lies."

I didn't believe the pain parasite business. He'd told me himself, in the Skeggy guest house, that it takes a liar to know another one, but I let it go. "Another thing, how could Julie Gahooley see you?"

"Practice. In her line of work she encounters weirder things than me."

"You're weird enough, but I suppose I should thank you for eighteen years of lies."

"You're welcome."

"So, now you've been found out, will you be moving on?"

"Not yet. You're still experiencing the pain of loss."

"Too right I am. I feel as if I've lost my dad all over again, and I've lost my job."

"Never mind. You didn't want to be an accountant anyway. Maybe Ginger-nut will come up with the career change he offered you."

I sighed. "I'm not holding my breath. I'll probably never hear from him again. During a holiday romance people say things they don't really mean."

"White lies?"

"Oh, shut up."

Three days later I was still half-heartedly job-seeking online. Nothing looked promising. Then Max's earrings were delivered by post. Hall-marked as silver, they each consisted of two fishes, both curled head to tail into a circle. The circles overlapped to form a vesica piscis, the symbol of perfect balance. I certainly needed that in my life. Recently I'd been teetering on the edge of a metaphorical cliff.

I called him. "The earrings are beautiful. Thank you. I don't deserve them for a quick sketch on the back of a tatty envelope."

"You're welcome. Listen, I've got a proposition for you." He told me he'd found business premises on the industrial estate north of the town. "I've got savings, but I'll need a bank loan as well. As soon as I've sorted it I'd love you to come and work for me."

"Yes, please. I won't have a clue what I'm doing, but I learn quickly, and you might not need a bank loan. My mum and my wayward dad have provided me with a nest egg and I need somewhere to invest it. Let's do it."

He laughed. "In that case you're not an employee, we're business partners."

"Fine by me, and if we need accountants I know a firm that owes me a favour."

"Emz, you're a star. Can I come over tomorrow and we'll get things moving?"

"Great. You can meet my mum. She'll like you. Come for lunch."

"Right, I'll bring cake. See ya."

Sophie Melancamp would have punched the air and whoo-hooed. I just closed my eyes and reveled in the moment. The earrings were working. Balance was being restored to my life.

When Mum came home from work I told her about Max's offer. She said, "Are you sure you can trust him?"

"Yes. Absolutely positive, I'm done with lies."

"In that case we'd better invite your Max to my wedding. Peter and I had lunch together today and we've set the date."

"About time. Invite Dad, with or without the chiropodist."

"Good idea. That's my other news. I had a letter from him this morning while you were still asleep. He wants to meet you."

We both cried a little and laughed a little, and I couldn't remember ever being happier.

That night the ghost said, "You can't feed me any longer." He looked more transparent than usual, and I knew I'd never see him again.

"I'll miss you," I said.

He shook his head. "No you won't, you'll have your live father back now."

I still wasn't sure I believed the pain parasite tale. Whoever the ghost was, perhaps he'd died in a plane crash on the way to Thailand. Who knows?

The ghost faded as he said, "Goodbye, Emily."

"Goodbye, Dad."

Ultimate Timeshare

JOCELYNE GREGORY

"If you ever want us to get married, you need to lose weight."

Donna peered over the rim of her sweetened iced coffee, swallowed the mouthful of acidic liquid and set her cup down on the faded green picnic table. They were a hundred feet from the welcoming sandy beach on the Peloponnesian, and the cool ocean breeze was a blessing from the Mediterranean summer sun.

"Excuse me? Frank, what did you just say?"

Frank sniffed the air, his lips turned downward, his designer sunglasses reflecting the bright sunlight. Sweat trickled down his brow, mingling with the expensive hair care products he spent on his rapidly receding hairline.

"You heard me," he said, his gaze on several women walking on the nearby sandy beach, their bikinis a combination of strings and scraps that left little to the imagination. When they passed, Frank glanced at Donna, her reflection clear in his sunglasses. "If you want us to get married, you need to lose weight. Think of the photos and social media posts. Plus, you'll need to be able to squeeze into your wedding dress."

Donna cleared her throat. She looked toward the beckoning waters and fought back the rising anxiety burrowing in her stomach. "You know my weight is a complicated subject."

"Then go see a shrink. Just know I'm not investing in a ring for someone who can't be bothered to take care of themselves."

"Right. Of course," Donna murmured. She looked at her half-drunk coffee and willed herself not to cry.

Frank pulled his phone from his pocket. "That Sparta tour starts in ten minutes. We need to leave now to get there early before the good spots are taken and the view is ruined by the tourists."

"Aren't we tourists too?" Donna muttered.

"We're influencers. Famous ones," he shot back.

Donna didn't reply. She followed Frank as they left the picnic table and walked the gravel road toward their next destination. He walked ahead of her, his collar popped, his pricey sandals threatening to snap from being used and not just displayed as part of a collection. He held his phone in hand, guiding them both toward their destination.

She looked out at the beach, her eyes drinking in the sparkling waters and straggly yet oddly familiar trees. A heavy sense of nostalgia weighed down her bones, and she was partially tempted to walk waist deep into the warm water and listen to the welcoming waves, but she could see Frank's sneering expression and his hurtful words. She shook her head and followed him as they walked inland and away from the beach's beckoning waves.

After several minutes of walking through oak and olive forest, along a narrow rocky path, a rambling creek and finally to a clearing rapidly filling with tourists, they arrived at their destination. Frank always walked faster than her, and this time Donna didn't try to keep up with his quick pace. She stung from his words earlier; not that they were the first, but she'd hoped they would be the last.

They'd come all the way to Greece to escape their busy lifestyles for a week, but all Frank had done was take selfies, talk on his Twitch channel to his viewers and show off the items his sponsors sent him. She'd been editing his videos since high school, and while he never allowed her to appear in them, he'd kiss her hands after a new video was posted, and the views climbed high in the top ten. It made sense they would be together...didn't it?

"Donna!"

"Frank?" She looked toward his voice and slowed as she spotted him standing with a pair of young women holding selfie sticks and giving their cameras picture perfect smiles. Frank waved her over, and she approached them, suddenly feeling self-conscious over her light dress, scarf and cardigan. Both women wore pastel-coloured activewear that clung to their slim bodies and barely left anything to the imagination.

"Ebriz, Alexia, this is my editor, Donna." Frank smiled at the two women.

"Oh my gosh, I was just telling Frankie how much I love the videos on his channel. The editing is masterful," Ebriz said.

Alexia nodded, her oversized straw hat nearly devouring her head. "It really is. And it's such a pleasure to meet someone who's so true to themselves in such a complex and overwhelming environment."

"You know, that's the way I like to live life. Every day is a new adventure, and I make sure that in my morning journal I note how blessed I am to be living a life of such authenticity and richness," Frank confessed, his hand pressed against his heart.

Donna bit the inside of her cheek and fought back the urge to roll her eyes. She turned her attention toward the growing number of tourists surrounding some old ruins of what looked like a small swimming pool.

"Donna, why don't you go check out that pool, and see if I can swim in it later," Frank whispered.

"It's an archeological site, I don't think you're allowed to," Donna said.

"I'm sure that as long as we respect and acknowledge the culture, it'll be fine," Frank soothed. "You should go ask; people love to help you."

It took Donna all of a minute before she pieced together his intentions as Alexia and Ebriz smiled and waved him over to join them for a short video.

"Sure. Because I'm the editor, right?" She hated how her voice cracked at the words.

"You're the best editor." Frank grinned. "I'll see you after the tour, okay? Alexia and Ebriz want to do a short cameo, you know, help boost their viewership."

"Of course," Donna muttered.

She walked away from Frank and the others, ignoring the hot whispers that burned her ears. She held her head up high; she wouldn't break down crying. She would cry later when she was alone in her *separate* hotel room.

Donna approached the group of tourists and gave a thankful smile to the people who made space for her. She examined the once beautifully carved stones and collapsed roof, the clear water and the partially obscured mosaic revealing half a woman's face with a blue eye and brown hair. She looked up to the tour operator, a sunburnt university student with a bright blue scarf holding back her neon red hair. Her eyes had that feral look all master students have when they get a chance to talk about their thesis projects uninterrupted.

"Allow me to introduce myself, I am your guide Antonia Farnese, and welcome to Hector's Pool! No, not that Hector from the Trojan War." She chuckled to herself. "But Prince Hector of Sparta of the experimental free colony that once existed here."

A tall woman raised her hand. "What makes this colony so special?"

"Good question! This specific colony was an experiment styled after a radical form of Greek philosophy where everyone was classified as citizens without the important Helot or the Perioikoi classes, the farmer or merchant classes that managed Spartan society. The Spartans wanted to know if this style of governance would work, and if people would be more willing to defend their homes and villages if they were citizens and all shared in governance and labour."

"Did it work?" A grey-haired British tourist asked.

"It did! For at least three-hundred years," Antonia explained. "But back to the star of the tour, Hector's Pool. According to local lore, dipping yourself in these waters can heal all ills and make your wishes come true. The healing part might be due to the naturally occurring sulphur in the water, but the wishes are another matter," she chuckled.

"Who built it?" Donna asked.

"Excellent question!" Antonia snapped her fingers. "This brings us back to Prince Hector. According to local legend, Prince Hector built this to honour the water nymph who called these waters home. This nymph was considered a great beauty, and an effigy of her image has slowly been uncovered in the bottom of the spring. Rumour is that Aphrodite was so jealous of this nymph's beauty and their love, that she banished the nymph and poor Prince Hector waited by the pool for the day she would return. Whether she did or not is left to history."

A soft murmur drifted across the crowd, and even Donna's heart panged. To think someone would love another so much they would wait a lifetime for them. Again, that strange sense of nostalgia for something she couldn't place washed over her like the ocean waves.

"Now, if you will all follow me over to that clearing, we will find the remains of the temple to the goddess, Artemis." Antonia herded the crowd in the direction of a roped off path that led to a small stone house in the woods.

Donna stayed behind, her gaze boring into the mosaic of the woman's face in the water. She didn't want to leave the pool.

The shrill cry of false laughter finally caused her to look back, and her heart sank as she watched Frank lean in and smile and laugh with Alexia and Ebriz. She bit her bottom lip and looked at the pool's clear water. It could grant wishes, couldn't it? It wasn't that she was desperate, well, it just was that she was desperate.

She pulled her camera from her bag and began taking pictures of the trees, the pool, the pathway and the environment. They would write off the vacation as a business expense of their business, Frank's business technically. She zoomed in on the mosaic within the pool and felt dizzy as she stared at the woman's blue eye.

"Donna?"

She glanced up from the camera and caught Frank's annoyed expression and the genuine concerned looks on Alexia and Ebriz's faces.

"Are you all right? Frankie's been calling you for a while." Alexia worried.

"I'm fine. Maybe the heat's gotten to me?" Donna gave a weary smile.

"You should take off that cardigan and scarf," Ebriz urged.

"Donna's one of those gentle souls who's still caught up in toxic beauty standards," Frank whispered conspiratorially.

She stared at Frank.

"But you look amazing," Ebriz gasped, drawing Donna's attention. "Don't listen to those haters, you be you and just bask in your radiance."

"Donna, I know we just met." Alexia clasped her hands to her chest. "But I feel like we share the same heart. Tomorrow the three of us can go out shopping and just have a girl's day, you know?"

"That's such a good idea." Ebriz nodded. "There are so many cute little shops, and I'm sure we can find you something stylish and light and embrace your body in the way it should be."

"And I can film just so you three can focus on having fun," Frank offered.

"Oh my gosh, Donna, you are so lucky to have someone as caring and thoughtful as Frankie." Alexia smiled.

Ebriz laughed. "She's so right!"

Donna smiled slightly, but she knew it didn't reach her eyes. "Thanks. I'll look forward to tomorrow. But I think I'm going to head back to the hotel. I think I'm getting too hot."

"You're scorching hot." Ebriz winked.

"I'll escort you back," Frank offered.

"No, no. You three stay." Donna waved him away.

"Oh, hey, before you go, excuse me." Frank pulled Donna away and leaned close. "Did you get the all clear to swim in the pool?"

Donna stared into Frank's grey eyes. "No. In fact, it's considered dangerous to swim in it. The water is loaded with high concentrations of arsenic and chemicals, and your skin will slouch off."

Frank's lips soured. "Really? We'll have to find another pool or lake or something. Viewers always love to see people play in the water."

"Especially with bikini-clad women," Donna muttered.

"Hey." Frank's grip tightened around her wrist. "Don't embarrass me tomorrow."

Donna yanked her wrist free and turned her back on Frank, Ebriz and Alexia. She walked on the empty trail, heading back towards the beach and the beckoning waves.

From the beach it was a quick walk to the hotel, and once inside her room, she shed her clothes and cooled off in a cold shower. When she finished, she towel dried her hair and wrapped another around her waist. She sat on the edge of her bed, her gaze distracted by the rolling waves of the ocean outside. She wasn't sure why she'd lied to Frank, but she didn't want to share the story of the tragic Spartan prince who waited for his love. She wiped away the tears because she knew Frank would never do that. More tears rolled down her cheeks as his comments came back to her, and the rolling waves drowned her sobs.

When the sun was setting, her phone lit up with a text from Frank telling her he was going to go out drinking with Ebriz and Alexia.

"Of course you are," Donna muttered to her phone.

Her stomach rumbled, reminding her to eat. She ignored it and grabbed her swimsuit, a dark iridescent blue one-piece with a high waist bottom and tummy control panel with a cute, scalloped back and plunging top that she knew made her breasts and ass look amazing.

She pulled on a loose maxi dress over her swimsuit and grabbed her phone and hotel key card. She walked along the beach, passing various tourists heading off to parties or their resorts. The waves grew louder and drowned out people's voices and the distant music of beach parties. She left the busyness of the modern world behind.

She retraced her path to Hector's Pool. She was careful not to trip on any rocks or branches as she slowly approached the collapsed ruins. Her heart began to beat faster and ached as she stood in front of the pool.

She checked her surroundings again. Certain she was alone, she set her phone and hotel key card aside and hesitantly pulled off her dress. She placed it on one of the broken pillars and dipped her toe into the waters. It was refreshingly cool. She eased herself into the water and gasped as she sank deep. She was surprised when her feet failed to touch the mosaic bottom, and she had to tilt her chin up to breathe. The smell of sulphur was faint. She drew in a deep breath and let it out.

"If this really is a wishing pool, then whoever is listening, please grant my wish," she whispered.

An owl hooted in the distance.

"I wish that Frank would love me as I love him, regardless of looks. I know his career is online, but there's more to love than meets the eye," Donna whispered.

Silence was her only response, and her heart sank as waves of anxiety and regret washed over her. She needed to speak from the heart. She squeezed her eyes shut as she spoke.

"Please," she whispered, fresh tears rolling down her cheeks. "I just wish to be with someone who will love me for me, and not for someone they want me to be."

Donna ducked her head under the water, and when she couldn't hold her breath anymore, she surfaced.

She wiped the water from her eyes and paused at the sight of the stars shining overhead, the sky pinkening with the morning sun. It was much later than she realized. A flicker of light in the distance caused her to panic.

"O—Oh, crap," she rasped. She turned in the pool, and for a disorienting moment she realized it was too dark to see anything. She ran her hand along the edges feeling for the stonework and touched grass and dirt instead.

The flickering light was coming closer, and Donna climbed her way out of the pool. She fumbled in the dark looking for her phone, dress and key card but only met stones, roots and nothing else.

"Where did they go?" she whispered.

"I hear a voice over here!" A man called out.

"Crap!" Donna bolted for the woods and hid behind an oak tree.

She clasped her hand over her mouth as two men entered the clearing from the path leading to Artemis's temple. The men were tall and carried torches, illuminating the spring and wore red cloaks wrapped around their bodies.

One of them gestured to the pool which looked nothing like the shrine Hector had built for his nymph. She swallowed as one of the men suddenly shed his red cloak to the ground leaving him partially naked; his exposed muscular bronzed skin exposed to the warm torchlight.

"Is this a hazing ritual?" She gasped. She stilled when both men looked toward her voice.

She slowly took a step back, and another as the men suddenly had short swords in their hands, and she bolted for the beach as the men chased after her. She stepped on pebbles and rocks alike. She cursed herself for not staying silent. Whatever she had stumbled upon was not her business, and given the men were chasing after her, she wasn't supposed to have seen it either.

The two men were quickly catching up to her but she could hear the reassuring waves of the ocean and the morning sunlight was helping her to find her way. If she could make it to the hotel, she would be safe.

She burst through the forest's edge and ran onto the beach, her mouth parting as she took in the brilliant morning light and the untouched sandy beach.

"There!" One of the men yelled behind her.

Donna ran for the ocean. She was a strong swimmer; she'd loved swimming, which was part of why she'd wanted to come here. Just before she reached the water, a spear landed right in front of her.

She froze, her eyes wide, taking in the nine-foot-long, bronze-tipped spear with a red piece of fabric trailing from the head. The thunderous sound of hoofbeats battled with the raging ocean's tide. A shadow blocked the sunlight, and she swallowed hard.

A man wearing a red cloak easily slid off the horse's unsaddled back. He towered over her, his bright eyes focused intently on her. He was tall with broad shoulders and black shoulder length hair braided away from his face. His beard was neatly trimmed on his strong jaw, and his lips thinned as he glared at her like she had done some great wrong.

"W—What do you want?" Donna stammered.

He stepped toward her, and she took a step back. The other horsemen were there too.

"She was near the spring," one said.

"You mean Hector's Pool?" she asked and took a double step backward as the man in front of her stepped closer.

He suddenly stopped, his intense eyes never leaving hers. "Orpheus, Ajax, stay back."

Donna realized they weren't coming toward her. She looked to the tall man in front, obviously their leader.

"Look, I don't know what's going on, or what you guys are doing, but it's none of my business. I just want to go home,"

Donna rambled.

"Toward the ocean?" The man tilted his head, his eyes glinting with the morning sunlight.

"I mean, the hotel? It's near the ocean?" she said.

"Sir, we can't let her leave," one of the men urged.

"What? Whoa, hold on, I didn't see anything! All right? I'm just a—a tourist here. Let me leave—"

The leader moved fast and grabbed her wrist, his hands calloused and hard.

"Let me go! Let me go!" Donna shrieked and tried to break free of his tight grip.

He wrapped his arm around her shoulder, his other wrapped around her waist, his fingers digging into the material of her swimsuit. He pressed her hard against his muscular body, and Donna gulped as he brought his face close to hers.

"You're going nowhere, nymph."

"Nymph?" she squeaked.

"Hector, be careful. Nymphs can seduce you," one of the men cautioned.

"Seduce?" Donna shrieked. "I'm not seducing anyone." She struggled in Hector's grip. "I am—I have a boyfriend! And I'm going to get married—someday. And besides, you're the one holding me! Let me go!"

Hector's grip tightened, and Donna quieted as he pressed his forehead against hers and stared into her eyes. She stared wide-eyed; her breath caught.

"Do you serve Poseidon? Or Aphrodite?" Hector

whispered.

"Who?" she whispered back.

He cocked his head, his eyes glinting with something that made her stomach clench and her heart hammer hard against her ribcage. "A wild born nymph, perhaps?"

"She came from the spring just like the priestess said she would," Ajax explained.

"And look at her clothing, she must have been sent by Aphrodite herself," Orpheus said.

"My swimsuit?" Donna's voice broke into a squeak as Hector suddenly picked her up as though she weighed nothing and placed her atop his horse. She grabbed the horse's long brown mane and clutched it tight as Hector joined her, one arm around her waist, the other grasping the reins.

"Orpheus, Ajax, return to the temple and ask the priestess to come to my home. I won't let this nymph out of sight." He kicked the horse's side.

Donna gasped as they rode hard and fast, and when the mane slipped from her fingers, she clutched the strong arm wrapped around her waist. The man, Hector, was an excellent rider even without a saddle. The strange sensation of riding a horse in her swimsuit was one she wouldn't soon forget.

"You must not be used to land horses," Hector said against her ear.

She fought back the shivers from his voice and tried to focus on what was going on around them, and ignore the fact that the rising sun was beautiful, and she couldn't see the hotel where it was supposed to be, or the public benches that normally dotted the coast.

"Where are you taking me?" she asked.

"Home."

"Where's home?" Donna tried to crane her head, but Hector's arm tightened around her waist. "Okay, Mr. Personality, who are you? And do you usually kidnap tourists?"

Hector gripped the reins and pulled the horse to a slow trot.

"Tourist? You provide tours for Poseidon or Aphrodite? No wonder the priestess said to keep you safe," Hector murmured.

"W—What?" Donna squawked. "No! I'm here on vacation with my boyfriend! Look, whoever you are, this has gone on too far, and I want answers!"

Hector pulled the reins again, and the horse stopped walking.

Donna gulped as Hector braced against her back and rested his chin on her shoulder. She could see the sharp angle of his nose from the corner of her eye, and the intense look in his eyes when he glanced back at her.

"I am Hector, sweet nymph."

"I'm not a nymph, I have a name," she hissed.

"And what is it, nymph?"

"It's Donna," she huffed.

"Donna?" He rolled the name around his mouth, his gaze turning distant and thoughtful. "Not technically Greek, closer to the language of those Etruscan upstarts, perhaps?"

"I'm from Minnesota," Donna whispered.

Their eyes met.

"Min—"

"Minnesota," Donna said slowly.

"Is that an Athenian province?" His brows furrowed.

"What? No, it's across the ocean in A—"

"Atlantis?"

"Do you say whatever comes to your mind while interrupting people before they can answer?" Donna said icily.

He cocked an eyebrow. "Only when people shriek, scream and try to escape back to their ocean homes, Nymph Donna."

"It's just Donna," she groaned.

"Come along, Nymph Donna. I suspect your kind doesn't like to be out of fresh water." He made a clicking sound with his tongue and the horse continued its way, albeit at a slower pace.

Donna scowled. Two could play at this game.

"And how are you so sure I'm a nymph and not a goddess?"

"If you were a goddess, Ajax and Orpheus would have been swept away by the tides, and I would have faced divine punishment for capturing you. No, you are a nymph. Your stubbornness and knowledge of foreign lands display Athena's gift of wit, and your voice is sweeter than siren song," he said.

She flushed at his words. He sounded sincere enough. She

couldn't remember the last time Frank complimented her on her voice.

She crossed her arms.

"Gorgeous view, if I may say so myself," Hector mused.

She blinked and looked down and blanched when she realized doing so pressed her breasts together and gave him a perfect view of the plunging neckline of her swimsuit. She immediately dropped her arms and grabbed the horse's mane instead. Heat blazed across her cheeks at his resulting chuckle.

"Shame," he said, "I know many a hero who's been seduced by a nymph's beauty, and I think I'm beginning to understand."

"I—I said I have a boyfriend!" she squawked.

"Boyfriend?" Again, Hector rolled the word. "He is your intended?"

"What? Well, technically, no? I mean, we've been together since school," she said.

"Ah, we have many of those relationships among our people," Hector mused. "Maybe we aren't as different as I originally thought. But, if he is your intended, where is he? And why were you unguarded without your goddess's protection? You do not appear a warrior."

"Are you saying I'm fat?" Donna said, her back stiffening.

Hector's grip tightened, and she blushed darker as he rubbed his thumb against her swimsuit covered side. "I am saying you have obviously been blessed by Aphrodite in all ways men, and women, find pleasant."

Donna swallowed. She fell silent, and as she realized they must be getting closer to the hotel and their meeting would end, she sighed. "My boyfriend doesn't find it pleasant."

The horse stopped again. It made an annoyed grumbling sound and flicked its head.

"You are a nymph of Aphrodite, and your intended looks down upon you? You were crafted by the goddess of beauty and love! Is that fool also in Minne-soota? Where is he?" Hector demanded.

"He—he went to a party with some other women?"

"Ah, he must be Athenian," Hector said. He clicked his tongue again and the horse continued its pace.

She glanced at the beckoning waves, and they approached what should have been the tall concrete building of the hotel. In its place was a small town with numerous houses, people wearing historical costumes like togas and tunics were milling about, chatting, and buying and selling in the day's market.

An icy chill ran up her spine as her mind struggled to realize the possibility that somehow everything was an elaborate prank, or she'd actually gone back in time to the freed town the history student mentioned.

"Where are we?" Donna whispered as they walked through the main thoroughfare past men of various ages on patrol, wearing red cloaks, over the shoulder togas and carrying shields and swords. She watched as the men tipped their heads to Hector before continuing, and she noticed several of the women gesturing to her and Hector.

"Home, Nymph Donna. The priestess, Antonia of Farnese said you were expected at the pool, and you would bring great prosperity to our village—and to me," Hector muttered the last part.

As if on cue, the doors of a tall wooden building opened and Antonia the master's student-slash-tour operator with the blue scarf wrapped around her neon red hair stepped out. Her eyes glinted with a wild knowledge, and she wore a colourful tunica with a slit up the side to expose her thigh and strapped sandals.

"You!" Donna shouted. She pointed her finger at Antonia, who had the grace to look slightly guilty. "You did this, didn't you!"

"I did nothing," Antonia defended. "It was the will of the goddess that brought you here."

"Wait. Let me off. Help," Donna squeaked. Hector helped her off the horse, and she stomped over to Antonia. "Where are we? What did you do?"

"This is the Spartan freed colony. And I didn't do anything; you heard the call of the pool, didn't you? Did you recognize yourself in the mosaic?" Antonia asked excitedly.

"I—wait, that's me?"

"Yes."

"Wait, that means he's Hector?" Donna pointed at Hector.

"He is." Antonia grinned.

"So, wait—"

"Shh." Antonia clamped her hand over Donna's mouth and leaned closer. "I know your boyfriend is an asshole, you didn't look happy at the tour, and Mr. Big the Strong Spartan soldier thinks you're a nymph sent by the goddess of love. You two are literally destined to be together."

"I have a life—" Donna began.

"Student loans? Credit card debt? Struggling to make ends meet? Asshole boyfriend that's going to leave you as soon as he finds some cute, young editor who'll fall for his bullshit?" Antonia asked.

Donna hesitated in answering.

"Look." Antonia wrapped her arm around Donna's shoulder. "You could go back to the future and your—Frankie was his name—or you could be worshipped as goddess-slash-nymph by a guy who already thinks you're wonderful. The Spartans? They love chatting and singing and fighting.

"Life isn't easy, but at least there isn't any social media to destroy your mental health."

"That's a horrible way to start a relationship," Donna hissed. "Wait, why are you here? What do you get?"

"Living archeology!" Antonia's grin widened, and that familiar graduate student's madness entered her eyes. "I'm going to bury a whole bunch of things, dig it up in the future, write my thesis, publish a few books, fake my death and come and live here as the priestess of Artemis. We're actually lucky; there is like zero archeological evidence of conflict, genocide, plague, or famine here for the next three-hundred years."

"If we've travelled back in time, how is it possible we speak their language?" Donna asked.

Antonia shrugged. "I think it's the magic pool."

Donna pursed her lips and glanced at Hector, who shamelessly winked at her. Her ears turned red, and she turned back to Antonia.

"So, my choices are…"

"Be worshipped like the goddess you are, playing on the beach, swimming, drinking, feasting and spending time with that stud. He's a prince and co-ruler of this colony, FYI, so you'll get more portions and better treatment. Or…"

"You're really good at this." Donna narrowed her gaze.

"And that's why I'm a priestess." Antonia laughed. "But look, choice is yours. You can go back, or stay. But you will need to leave eventually for Hector to build the pool for you so you can come back here," Antonia explained, her expression turned serious.

Donna glanced at Hector again. He appeared deep in discussion with several older men wearing long tunics.

"So, the pool has a happy ending?" Donna asked, surprised.

"Up to you." Antonia shrugged. "It's your choice."

"My choice," Donna murmured.

Most of her life choices since high school consisted of following Frank around and doing everything she could to please him in the hopes he would look at her and appreciate her hard work without a backhanded compliment or a snide comment. She had gone into the pool wishing to meet someone who would love her for her, and in response she had been magically teleported back to Spartan times and met Hector. Maybe the gods really did grant her wish.

"Hector!" Donna called out.

"Nymph Donna?" Hector suddenly straightened.

She parted her lips to speak, but her voice caught in her throat. His brown eyes shined with warmth, and he ignored the village elders that crowded around him. He stared at her like what she said next were the most important words in history. Her heart ached at the way he looked at her, and for a moment she thought of the life she would leave behind, and the potential life she would have with Hector.

Antonia was right. Donna had more than enough pressures in her life. Her holiday was supposed to be a chance to relax and rebuild her relationship with Frank, but did she really want to be with him? She would miss modern conveniences of her life back in Minnesota, but she desperately wished to be looked at like the way Hector looked at her.

If she stayed, she wouldn't be alone. And Antonia said the village would be safe for several centuries. And if things didn't work out with Hector, she could always leave and return to the modern world. The choice was hers, and she wanted to give the handsome Spartan prince who thought she was a nymph sent by the goddess Aphrodite a chance.

The eyes of the village focused on her, and she let out a small, nervous smile.

"I'll stay."

Hector grinned, his intense eyes lighting with her words. He turned to the surrounding crowd. "You heard the nymph! She stays!"

Lemon Drops at Mermaid Lagoon
LEIGH CALVIN

"What do you mean my room won't be ready until eight p.m.? Are you sure it's my room that isn't ready? You put in the correct name? Rayna Levin?"

I say this as nicely as I can despite the fact I'm trying not to freak out. My flight was delayed, traffic was awful getting to the resort, I am sweating to death because I haven't been able to change out of my Philadelphia cold weather clothes, and I am starving. Starving!

Okay, deep breath. I put my best "truly, I'm a lovely customer" smile on and wait to hear why my confirmed for three p.m. today room is not ready at what is now four p.m. What could be the problem? I'm hoping whatever it is gets sorted out before my sister arrives from North Carolina for our sisters' weekend. If she gets here (and by the way, why isn't she here already; her flight was supposed to land first) and we don't have a room, she's going to be annoying. My sister Alex tends to be dramatic, and I am really not in the mood. I want our weekend to be calm and peaceful so we can catch up and have lots of quality sister time.

The somewhat frazzled young woman at check-in cringes and continues, "It's just that we seem to be short-staffed, and housekeeping has several rooms to clean before yours. I'm really, really sorry."

"Isn't there anything you can do? Can you switch around the order the rooms are getting cleaned? Maybe give me a different room? What am I supposed to do with myself and my luggage for four hours?"

I clearly must look somewhat pitiful because the front desk clerk sighs and says, "Hold on…" She starts typing up a storm, then stops and tells me she'll be right back. I am crossing all my fingers and toes that she's going to come back with good news.

The clerk looks noticeably happier as she approaches her station and me. With a big smile she says, "I spoke to the manager and explained the situation. The only room that would be available before eight p.m. is one that would be available at six p.m. I know that's not great, but this room is a suite, and the manager said we could upgrade your room for free to make up for the inconvenience. She also said to comp your meal if you want to go over to our restaurant and have a bite to eat while you wait. I can have the bell person hold your luggage and then bring it up to your room when it's ready." The clerk, who can't be more than twenty-two or twenty-three, and is tiny and adorable, smiles up at me, very pleased with herself. I think she would high-five herself if I weren't looking.

Okay, six p.m. is not great, but it's better than eight p.m., and the room upgrade and food seems like a pretty fair trade. I smile back at her, thank her for taking care of the problem and accept her offer. She hands me a card from the manager that tells me my meal will be comped at The Mermaid Lagoon, their waterfront eatery. This is at least perfect; Alex and I are supposed to meet up at the bar there. We figured it would be better than one of us hanging out bored in the lobby waiting.

After she hands me a resort map and tells me how to find my way to the restaurant, I leave my coat, sweater and luggage with her and head outside. Jeans and a t-shirt are still a little warm for eighty-five-degree weather, but it's definitely better without my coat and sweater.

I walk around a little and land at The Mermaid Lagoon, which as it turns out is not a lagoon nor are there mermaids. I grab a corner seat at the bar where I can see the door to watch for my sister. I order a lemon drop martini, (please make it the right way) and ask to see a menu. I figure I'll have Alex meet me here when she arrives. I'll text her and let her know what's going on and where I am. I pull out my phone and see I have missed four calls from her, two from her husband Ryan and a voice mail. I also have about four hundred texts from her. This cannot be good. Before I can even listen to her message or read the texts my phone rings, and I see it's her.

"Hey, Alex! What's going on? I just checked my phone and saw I have a bunch of stuff from you. I was about to see what's up but now you're calling me. So, where are you? Is everything okay? Was your flight delayed? Are you on your way here now? Wait! Are you here?" There is no sound from the other end. "Hello? Can you hear me?" I ask.

"I was just waiting to make sure you were finished," she says in that older sister way she has. "It didn't seem like you were ever going to stop talking."

Ugh. Rude. I roll my eyes, take a sip of my drink (oh my God, it's perfect, yay!) and say "Sorry, I'm finished. I'm just excited and can't wait for you to get here."

"I'm not coming."

"What? What do you mean you're not coming?"

My outburst causes a few people to turn around and see who is yelling in the middle of a restaurant. I try to appear menacing, hoping I am giving a "mind your own business" look to whoever is looking and then refocus on my sister.

The guy on the other side of the bar catches my eye and gives me an amused smile. What is that about? There is nothing amusing going on. He is handsome enough though that I do a double take, which makes him chuckle and shake his head a little at me. I wonder if I can throw the lemon slice from my drink at him. It might be too far, so maybe not a great idea. I don't want to accidentally hit the bartender. Plus, at fifty years old it might come off as a bit less mature than what I'm going for.

I don't want to give off an unhinged, middle-aged divorcee vibe, so I leave my lemon slice where it is and go back to listening to my sister. I'll just quietly hope that Mr. Amused's drink spills on his lap. Yes, I'm petty. Whatever.

I get off the phone after my sister explains that while she was at the airport, she tripped over her rolling carry-on, (how did she even do that) and then before she could move to get up, some giant football player-looking guy tripped on her suitcase and then fell on her. She has two broken ribs and a sprained wrist. She said she'll be fine but is in pain and obviously can't make it to Florida. I tell her not to worry, that I'm not mad, and that I'll be fine spending the weekend alone. Before we hang up, she asks if I am already at the bar. I say that I am. I'm not sure why, but she seems relieved. I don't really give it much thought because I am already trying to figure out what I'm going to do for three and half days by myself. I tell her I'm sorry that she's hurt and that I'll miss her. I hope she's believing the cheery "It's fine" attitude that I'm not really feeling.

Since I am having a horrible day, I order another drink, (where did the rest of that first one go?) and a fried chicken sandwich with cheese and bacon. Since I am stressed and using alcohol and food to help de-stress, said food and drink is therapeutic, and therefore "health food." Trust me. It is.

My food arrives as I finish drink number two. Not wanting to have to stumble to my room, I decide to switch to club soda (because, mature). At this point I am ravenous and tear into my sandwich. First bite, big giant sigh, and a moan. It is so good! Maybe I'm just really hungry, but still, yum!

I'm so focused on my food and scrolling through my phone, that I don't notice that Mr. Amused has made his way over to my spot at the bar.

"I was really hoping to see what would happen after a third drink."

I look at him and blink a couple times thinking it will help me understand what's going on right now. Nope, it didn't help.

"Are you serious? Who says that to a stranger? And why do you know how many drinks I've had? You do know that's kind of creepy and weird, right? I bet there are cameras in here. If I end up dead in a dumpster, they'll know it's you. I didn't plan time in my vacation schedule to be murdered."

Dead silence. Then he chuckles at me again and just stands there smiling. "Maybe it's better you don't have that third drink."

I'm a little torn at this point. On one hand I want to tell him if this is how he tries to talk to a woman he meets at a bar, it's no wonder he's single (we're going to hope that's the case). On the other hand, he's really *really* good looking: salt and pepper hair, light blue eyes, tall and fit and appears to be age appropriate. I kind of like that he's talking to me. He also one hundred percent has the smolder thing going on, which is hot.

Don't get me wrong, I have no issue with my looks, but being short (my sister insists five foot three is short, but she's mean), middle-aged, on the curvy side, and more cute than beautiful, I can't imagine I'm the type of woman this guy usually hits on. I picture him going for tall, blonde and beautiful. But he did walk over here, and since I have a lot of time to kill and no sister here to talk to or to stop me from, in her words, "constantly scaring away perfectly nice men," I decide I will forgive his initial rudeness and see where things go.

So, I give him my "bless your heart smile" and then look over toward the bartender and say, "I've changed my mind. I think I *will* have another drink." And, because I am delightful and generous, I turn back towards Mr. Amused and ask, "Can I buy you a drink?" (I am mentally high-fiving myself for being such a sophisticated, modern woman.)

He smirks again at me and says, "No thanks, I'm good," and then just stands there looking at me.

I look at him with some confusion and admittedly some embarrassment, shrug and say, "Suit yourself. Why did you come over here if you don't want to hang out and have a drink?"

"I didn't say I didn't want to hang out, I said I didn't want a drink."

"Oh."

He then holds out his hand and introduces himself, "Zach Campbell. Welcome to The Mermaid Lagoon." I must look confused because he adds, "This is my restaurant."

Again, I cleverly respond with, "Oh."

"Does that make you more or less concerned about me murdering you?"

I snort (ugh, not sexy) and smile, liking that he's going along with my silliness/concern about being murdered. "Hmmm, I guess less. It's probably not good for business if you go around killing your customers."

He smiles for real this time (and oh my god he is really handsome) and says, "No, I guess it wouldn't be."

"I thought the restaurant was owned by the resort?"

"They own the space; I lease it. The restaurant has to follow some resort guidelines, but other than that I'm free to do things how I want. I really wanted to create a casual, beachy place where you could roll in wearing whatever and feel comfortable. I also wanted the food to be fun and special, not your typical resort fare."

"Are you a chef?" I ask.

"No, but I was able to find a great executive chef who was willing to collaborate with me on the menu."

"That's pretty cool. How did you get into the restaurant business? Are you here full time? Are you busy all day managing things? Do you ever get tired of dealing with snooty resort guests? Wait! You don't think I'm one of those, do you? Oh no! You do, don't you?"

"How about you let me ask some questions now?" he says as he smiles at me. It seems like he's been smiling at me the whole time he's been over here. It's making it hard to concentrate on the conversation. I'm worried I'm staring. (Being halfway into my third drink, it's likely I am.) I'll assume the alcohol is why my stomach is all fluttery. Yes, I'm sure that's it.

"First question is what's your name and second question is do you always ask forty-seven questions at once before someone can even answer the first one?"

"One, Rayna Levin. Two, I can't help it if I have a lot of questions. I like to get up to speed on things right away. You can never be too prepared in any situation."

"Rayna's a pretty name. Not one I've heard before."

"My friends call me Ray—like ray of sunshine," I say, very pleased with the new nickname I just gave myself. (What? He's a stranger, he doesn't know.)

"No they don't." He gives me a look that says he knows I just made that up.

"You don't know. Maybe they do. Okay, fine, they don't. My sister does sometimes call me Death Ray. She says I kill the vibe when I go on a ramble, which she says scares people—specifically men—away. She's rude."

"You don't get along with your sister?"

"Oh no, I do. She's the best. It's just that as the older sister she feels compelled to offer me her 'help' even when I don't want it. I was supposed to be spending the weekend with her. We even tacked on today to make it a longer weekend. I flew in from Philadelphia, and she was coming from North Carolina."

"Why aren't you?"

"Why aren't I what?"

"Why aren't you spending the weekend with her?"

"She got hurt at the airport and can't come. Don't even ask. And, when I got here, I was informed my room wouldn't be ready for hours. The hotel is upgrading my room and is paying for my meal here as an apology, so that's good, but I'm not thrilled to be spending my vacation money to hang out by myself. I could have done that at home for free."

"Huh, that's funny. A buddy of mine from college was supposed to be coming for the weekend, but he called earlier today to say that work had given him a new case to handle. It's a great opportunity for him to impress the big wigs, so he felt like he couldn't get away. He's trying to become a partner in the firm where he recently started working."

"That's a bummer, I'm sorry. At least you're at home. Wait. Do you actually live here at a resort!? I'm so jealous. Is it awesome? Do you get to hang out at the pool or beach every day? Do you get free umbrella drinks since you own the place?"

This turns his smile into an outright laugh. "I'll tell you what," he says. "Since we both are now flying solo, why don't you come back here around eight p.m. or so, and you can sit at the bar and have dinner and keep me company. Once my friend canceled, I let Ethan, (he points to the bartender) have the night off, so I'll be working the bar. I'll answer all your questions then." He says all this while taking my hand.

(Oh my god oh my god oh my god, be cool. Do NOT giggle and blush like you are fourteen. You are a sophisticated fifty-year-old woman. Sophisticated! Try not to act like you've never spoken to another human before and say something. Stop staring and answer. But, jeez, just him holding my hand is making me all dizzy and tingly. Well, it's that or the three drinks. I'm sure it's the drinks. I have never been the swoony sort.)

Finally, I gather my wits (well, what there is left of them) and answer, "Wow! That'd be great. Thanks for the offer. It will be nice to not spend the whole evening alone. Can you make a lemon drop as good as Ethan can?"

Zach just shakes his head at me and says, "Guess you'll have to find out for yourself. I have to head into the kitchen to make sure everything is good to go for the dinner shift before I can send Ethan on his way. I'll save your seat at the bar. You'll be in a great spot for people watching when I can't talk to you. You'll also be in a great spot for me to watch you." Then he winks at me. (Breathe. Breathe. He winked at you; he didn't take off his clothes.) Thinking about him with no clothes is not helping. I head to the door as he heads for the kitchen. Suddenly I remember I didn't give him my voucher from the front desk.

"Wait! I forgot to pay. I have a voucher."

"We'll settle up later. See you soon."

I turn back around to leave, and I trip. Over nothing. Over air. Really?! I am praying Zach did not see that, but of course he did. I hear him call behind me, "Don't worry, Rayna Levin, I didn't see a thing." I don't even turn around. Just shake my head and keep moving.

Thankfully, I get checked in and escorted up to my suite with no further issues. I wasn't thrilled to see the après-plane look I was sporting by the time I arrived in my room. Frizzy hair, smudgy mascara, general rumpledness. The up-side being if Zach saw me like that and was still interested, then good for me. I wasn't sure which outfit to choose, but anything would be an improvement over my sweaty plane clothes.

Closer to eight-thirty, then eight, I head down to The Mermaid Lagoon (I will have to discuss the lack of mermaids or lagoons with Zach). I got my wavy medium length brown hair to behave and the turquoise sleeveless sundress I chose showed off my curves without being clingy. The nude sandals I wore were perfect with the dress. I had put on some mascara and lip gloss, and I was happy with how I looked. Zach is absurdly handsome, and it was making me a little insecure, but I didn't want to look like I was trying too hard to impress him. He was going to either like me or he wasn't. I was hoping he did.

The restaurant is crowded, and I have to wade through a bunch of people to get into the bar area. Zach had his back to me and is making drinks. It was like he knew I walked in because right away he turns around, nods, and points to "my spot" at the bar. I smile and head over to my seat. Before he turns back to making drinks, he winks at me. It was a sexy "hey there" wink, not an "I have something in my eye or a nervous twitch" wink. Thank God he stops looking at me because the urge to giggle and flutter my lashes comes over me again. Good lord, it's not like the first time I've ever interacted with a handsome man. Maybe the giggle urge is some symptom of menopause that was just now starting to plague me. Slightly embarrassing, but way better than the hot flashes where I feel like I am being microwaved from the inside out. Though, now that I notice, I am feeling a little warm. And, not in a menopause kind of way.

When Zach gets a reprieve from drink making, he comes over to me and takes my hand again. Without looking away from my face, he turns my hand over and starts to rub his thumb back and forth on my palm and the inside of my wrist. "Hi," he says, "I'm glad you came. I was worried you'd decide to just order room service."

"Nope," I reply. "I couldn't pass up the opportunity to see if you can win the lemon drop challenge."

"What do I win if mine is better than Ethan's?" he says in a low voice and jokingly waggles his eyebrows at me. Before I could think of something clever to say, he hands me a menu and asks me if I wanted any suggestions. "I want you to have something that will make you sigh and moan like the chicken sandwich did." Several inappropriate comments come to mind all at once, none of which I should say out loud. I must have looked dumbstruck because Zach starts to laugh as he walks away to make my drink and says over his shoulder, "Breathe, Rayna. You look like you're biting your tongue. Was there something you wanted to say?"

"There was not." I say in a way that makes it clear that we are not about to have this conversation. I am not usually this dorky and awkward. (I don't know, maybe I am, and I just hadn't noticed until now. Nope. If I was, my sister would have one hundred percent told me already.)

The drink is delicious. I tell Zach it is the same caliber as Ethan's, so there's no winner, thus no prize. He then jokingly calls me a coward. I disagree and tell him he's a poor sport. We both smile and laugh. In the few hours I've known him I feel like we've done nothing but smile and laugh. (Of course, he was laughing at me earlier and not with me, but I am choosing to ignore that part.)

I order the Cajun salmon over a corn risotto with asparagus. While I wait, Zach and I get to know each other a bit in between drinks he has to make. He's fifty-five, divorced for a long time, and has a twenty-six-year-old daughter who lives nearby and is a third grade teacher. He told me he has always worked in the restaurant business in one way or another, both in the front and back of the house. He has a little cottage on the resort property where he's lived for the last three years.

I tell him that I am also divorced and that I hadn't gotten married until I was thirty-five and was divorced by forty. There is nothing awful about my ex, we just weren't a good fit. We didn't have kids, and without a partner I didn't feel like it was something I wanted to do on my own. I work as a travel writer for a high-end travel company, and I am always flying off somewhere for a few days to check out the newest hot spots. That lifestyle has started to wear on me, and I have been contemplating my next step. That is part of the reason my sister and I were having a girl's weekend. She was going to help me go through my options.

When my salmon comes Zach pours me a glass of white wine and watches as I take the first bite. It's delicious and my eyes close and the food moan sneaks out before I can stop it. Maybe the floor will open up and swallow me. I slap my hand over my mouth, but he pulls it away, the corners of his mouth tilting in amusement, and keeps holding my hand and staring at me. He quietly says, "Don't. I like that you're enjoying it. Plus, now I can tell my friend that I didn't miss him at all this weekend because I was busy making a woman moan." The last part breaks the tension which was definitely getting a little thick.

"Shut up! Don't tell him that." I say half-heartedly because it was pretty funny. But I also like that it seems I finally made him feel as off kilter as he's been making me. "So, you said this was a college friend. Where did you go to college? What was your major? How did you and your friend meet? Were you roommates?"

"And the 'Ray of sunshine' is back," he says with a wink.

"Ha ha, hysterical."

"We met at freshman orientation at Penn State." He tells me.

"Cool. My sister and brother-in-law both went there. That's where they met."

"My friend met his wife at school too. I guess it's not that uncommon. What're your sister and brother-in-law's names?"

"Alex and Ryan Taylor." Before I can ask his friend's name, he stares at me like my hair is on fire and shakes his head a couple times in disbelief. "What's wrong?" I ask.

"Uh, I think we have friends who have some explaining to do." He says while softly laughing to himself and continuing to shake his head. I tilt my head and raise my eyebrows and gesture for him to clarify.

"The friend who was supposed to visit me *is* Ryan Taylor. His wife's name is Alex. When he said he wasn't coming he didn't mention his wife got hurt or that she had been planning on being here too."

As I think of all the ways I am going to maim my sister (after of course I tell our mother on her, because-are you kidding me right now) I look at Zach and say, "I can't believe they did this! She didn't mention Ryan was supposed to be coming. I bet she's not even hurt! I bet she didn't even buy a plane ticket! Was this all a setup? I can't believe she was willing to risk me being alone all weekend. What if we never met? What if we met but didn't like each other? She is dead to me. We are not speaking." I angrily pick up my phone and start dialing Alex's number. Before I can finish, Zach pulls my hand away from the phone.

"I do like you."

"What?" I ask.

"I do like you," he says quietly. "I hope you're okay with that. I'd love if we could hang out this weekend."

The hottest guy I have ever spoken to likes me and wants to hang out with me. I think I just swallowed my tongue.

"Don't swallow your tongue," he says while smirking at me.

"Oh my god!! I can't believe I said that out loud! I thought I only said it in my head! See what my sister has done to me? Her evilness has addled me."

"You think I'm hot?"

"That's your takeaway here?!"

"Pretty much," he says pseudo-smugly. He can see I'm a little bit embarrassed to have blurted that out, so he adds, "well, here's a takeaway for you. I think you're hot too."

"You do not! You're just saying that so I won't go throw myself in the ocean."

"No," he says sincerely, "I do think you're hot. I think you're also smart and funny. I haven't been able to look away from your beautiful green eyes, and I love all that wavy brown hair. And those curves...they're killer. I almost followed you out of here earlier today when you left."

Being the cool cucumber I am, I just sit there staring at him.

"Tell you what," he adds, "I'm off tomorrow. Let's figure out a plan to make them think they've caused a disaster and that we hated each other on sight. Until then, we say nothing."

"That's perfect! My sister will definitely be texting me and asking "innocent" questions trying to feel out the situation. I won't even answer. She can worry that I'm dead in a ditch somewhere."

"Even though she knows you don't have time in your vacation schedule to get murdered?" he asks.

I roll my eyes at him and make a face. "Shut up. I actually don't have time to get murdered."

At this point I notice the restaurant is mostly empty, with just a few patrons finishing up their drinks at the bar. I check my watch. "Wow! I didn't realize how late it is."

"You must be tired. It's been a long day for you. We don't

officially close until midnight, but it's empty enough that we can start cleaning up and prepping for tomorrow. Then, once I let the staff go, I have some paperwork to finish up. Hopefully, I'll be out of here by one-ish."

"That's a long day for you, too."

"I'm used to it. Besides, like I said, I'm off tomorrow, so I can sleep in." He wipes his hand on a bar towel and comes around to my side of the bar. "Let me get a server to finish up with the last bar customer, and I'll walk you to the hotel. Then I can come back and finish up."

"I'm fine on my own. I don't want you to be here even later."

"I don't want you to walk alone in the dark and besides, I'm not quite ready to say good night yet. Just wait here for a second." Then he leans in and gives me a gentle kiss. Smiling, he puts a finger up to indicate he'll be back in a minute and disappears into the kitchen.

It was just a quick kiss, but my lips are tingling. Honestly, all of me is tingling. From just one kiss. Sigh. All that is going through my head now is when Phoebe teased Monica, "My boyfriend is ever so dreamy." (I know he's not my boyfriend, well, maybe he will be, but he's not yet. I like him, he seems into me, and he's really handsome. And, oh my god, if that little kiss was any indication, I really want to see what a "real" kiss will be like.)

He holds my hand as we walk toward the hotel. He asks my room number and we head up. When we get to my door, I thank him for walking me back. We make a plan to meet in the lobby at eleven a.m. the next day for brunch and revenge planning. I'm not quite so sad I'm here without my sister.

"I wish we could hang out more. I hate that I have to head back to the restaurant," he says, facing me as I lean back against my door. He takes the key from me and opens my door. I'm about to say goodnight and go in, but he gently nudges me in and follows and closes the door.

"I thought you have to go."

"I do. But I wanted to kiss you goodnight, and it didn't seem hallway appropriate."

"It didn't?"

"No. It did not." Then, before I can say anything further, I see why he didn't think it was hallway appropriate. He pushes me up against the inside of my door. One of his hands is in the back of my hair and the other is on my waist and he leans in and kisses me. At first, it's gentle like in the bar, but then his tongue runs across the seam of my lips until I open, and he's licking into my mouth, coaxing my tongue with his. My arms come up around his waist, and I run my hands up his back. He moves my hands around his neck and deepens the kiss. Then his hands are roaming up and down my body. He leaves my mouth to kiss my neck and down to my collar bone. While his mouth heads back up to mine he runs his hands up my front, caressing my breasts. I have never been kissed like this before. For the first time in my life, I don't think there are any words running through my head. I can only focus on kissing him and what his hands are doing to me. I can feel this kiss down to my toes. I think the only reason I am still upright and not a puddle on the floor is that he is holding me up against the door. I don't think I am breathing. (I mean I must be, but I can't tell.)

Zach pulls back, and I have to admit I'm feeling very pleased with myself that he seems to be as affected by our kiss as I am. He just stands there for a minute smiling down at me.

"See. Not hallway appropriate."

I chuckle quietly and reply, "No, it certainly was not. I think I like hallway non-appropriate. A lot."

"Me too."

"I really wish you didn't have to leave," I whisper.

"Me too," he says again.

He leans down and gives me one last lingering kiss. "I'll see you tomorrow. Sweet dreams."

I sigh. "You too. Good night."

He leaves, and I close the door and put the safety lock on (don't want to be murdered, remember). I just stand there with my back against the door, smiling like a loon. Even when I go to wash up and brush my teeth, I see myself still smiling in the mirror.

I cannot wait for tomorrow.

Mermaid and Coyote
ROSE STRICKMAN

On the first day of his early retirement, Alejandro drove down to the coast, humming in time to the radio and looking out for the first sight of the sea.

So far, early retirement was a blast. Alejandro found everything about the coastal highway ten times more beautiful and interesting than before—from the dusty chaparral, to the old houses clinging to the hillsides, to the sycamores growing along the waterway at the floor of the valley. Even Coyotl was happy, rejoicing in the feast of sights and smells. When he topped the final row of hills and beheld the Pacific Ocean, Alejandro laughed aloud with pure delight and Coyotl yipped in glee.

Alejandro zipped and swerved along the highway, circling ever downward, until at last he reached sea level. At the first opportunity, he pulled off down a side road from the highway, curving toward a small cove.

Alejandro cut the engine. In the ensuing silence, he could

hear the murmur of the waves rolling in. Coyotl scratched at his mind, begging him to get out.

He unbuckled his seatbelt and opened the door. The voice of the ocean swept over him, the continual song of the waters. He closed his eyes and listened, breathing deep of the ocean's scent, Coyotl dancing with delight, before swinging himself out of the car.

He was alone by the tiny bay, save for a single beat-up car parked some distance off. There was some sand, overgrown with beach grass, but the shore here was rocky; the waves struck great slabs and boulders, washing off in foamy white waterfalls. Alejandro admired the ocean's power, the shining blue under the clear sky, before heading down for a closer look.

It was low tide. Weeds hung off the edges of the boulders, barnacles had their shells tight closed. There were sea anemones folded up, and sea stars clinging to the rocks. Alejandro admired the sea life and meandered the shore, letting Coyotl get his fill of scents—then stopped short.

It seemed the owner of the strange car admired this view too. She stood on a large, flat shelf of rock, just above the reach of the waves, her easel standing before her. Biting her lip with concentration, she dipped her brush and added another wash of color.

Alejandro stood back and admired the view. She was a beautiful woman, tall and graceful, her strawberry blonde hair held back in a messy bun, strands lifted by the wind. Her face was stained delicately red from that same sea wind, and her hand, lifting her brush, was long and slim.

Inside his mind, Coyotl's attention pricked. He started dancing, tongue hanging out. Coyotl, too, liked the look of this woman.

Alejandro considered announcing himself—it wasn't every day he met a beautiful woman by the sea—but she seemed deeply absorbed in her painting. It would be better to leave her to her work.

At that moment, as though she heard his thoughts, the woman looked up.

Alejandro found himself staring into a pair of vivid blue-green eyes, the color of a transparent sea with the sun shining through it, framed by long golden lashes. He opened his mouth, but whatever he intended to say drowned in the waters of those eyes, lost forever at sea.

"Hi!" said this goddess, grinning.

Alejandro managed to hoist his jaw up. "Hi." Within, Coyotl whined with lust and eagerness; Alejandro forced him down.

"Admiring the view?" The woman gestured at the rocks, the sun and the sea.

"Oh, yes," said Alejandro, honestly enough.

"It *is* beautiful, isn't it?" The woman turned back to gaze happily at the sea.

Alejandro still felt half-blinded by her gaze. He came closer, only half-conscious of his decision to do so, climbing down over the rocks, Coyotl panting in his mind. The painting came into better view.

"Oh, wow..." The painting wasn't just an average oceanscape. It was the ocean, all right, but under the waves, as though in an aquarium, a group of sea lions swam among tall, swaying kelp, chasing fish and trails of silver bubbles. The style was very familiar...

Then he had it. "Hey—are you Elena Seagraves?" he blurted out.

"That's me!" The painter grinned again. "Do you know my work?"

"Know it? I love it! I've got one of your mermaid pictures at home." Alejandro stared at her avidly. Elena Seagraves was famous for her self-portraits depicting herself as a mermaid, the reddish-golden scales of her tail matching her long hair adrift in the water.

"Which one?" Elena put her paintbrush behind her ear, a movement that fascinated Alejandro—and Coyotl.

He jerked out of the paintbrush-induced haze and pushed down Coyotl. "The one with you swimming with great whites."

"Well, they're very misunderstood creatures, you know," she said.

"Yes, they are." At this point, Alejandro would have agreed with anything she said, on any topic. "You're really into ocean conservation, aren't you? I've donated to your nature fund."

"Thank you! Fifteen percent of all painting sales go to removing plastic from the ocean, you know. The more you buy, the more you save!" Elena grinned sheepishly. "Sorry.

That's super cheesy."

"No, it's not. I think it's great what you're doing…"

They stood and talked, completely absorbed, while the sun sank down toward the sea and the tide started creeping up the rocks. It was only when the first wave darted up to wash around the easel's legs that the spell was broken. Elena yelped and snatched her painting up. Alejandro dived to save the easel.

"Maybe we should continue this conversation on dry land," Elena suggested with a laugh. "There's this great indie coffee house in town. The Bucket. I can lead you there in my car."

Looking into her eyes, Alejandro had that sensation again, that he was drowning, with no desire ever to rise to the surface. "Yes," he heard his own voice saying. "Yes."

Coyotl's yowl of approval echoed through Alejandro's thoughts.

Alejandro helped load Elena's equipment back into her car, then followed her in his own car to the edge of the town of Santa Rosales, where the bucket-shaped sign of The Bucket loomed. The coffee house was just as good as advertised. Elena and Alejandro sat in a booth overlooking the garden, cups steaming before them. They spent so long talking, and had such absorbing conversation, that Alejandro was surprised when the coffee house's staff members started flicking the lights on and off.

He looked up, blinking. "Guess that means it's time to go." Outside, a long, languorous summer evening was settling over the coffee house garden, golden as Elena's hair.

"Yes." Elena had an odd, faraway look. "Yes, I think the tide's going out again."

"Do you know the local tides so well?" Alejandro was intrigued.

Elena seemed to come back to herself, giving that wonderful smile. "You could say so."

"Wow!" Alejandro looked at his phone and let out a sigh of exasperation and annoyance. "Damn. I've missed the sign-in time for my rental!"

"Well..." Elena's smile turned sly. Her hand snaked out to touch Alejandro's. "You know, I've got some extra space at my place. If you'd like."

Coyotl rubbed himself ecstatically against Elena's touch. Alejandro felt an answering grin spread across his own face. "Thanks, Elena. I'd like that very much."

They sat, grinning stupidly at one another, until the manager swung by to start banging chairs onto tables while simultaneously glaring and smirking at them.

Elena's house was a beautiful cottage overlooking the sea. "I inherited it from my mom," Elena explained, helping Alejandro carry his luggage into the house. "I could probably sell it for six million dollars now. But I'd never give it up." She smiled fondly around the small, cozy living room.

Alejandro breathed deep of the scent of sea salt and an attractive woman. Coyotl slavered. *Down, boy.*

"I don't blame you." It really was a nice house, he thought: small, but scrupulously clean, the walls hung with art, rooms arranged with comfortable furniture, all the colors complementing. But right now Alejandro didn't care about the house so much. Coyotl was practically tearing his subconscious to shreds with eagerness and frustration, and Alejandro wanted nothing more than to give the beast his head.

It seemed Elena had similar ideas. She turned to Alejandro with a hopeful light in her eyes. "So...we could have dinner."

"Yeah. I guess we could." In Alejandro's mind, Coyotl screamed in protest at the idea.

"Or..." Elena stepped closer, then closer still. "...Not."

"Not," Alejandro gasped, and then there was very little need to talk.

The next morning, Alejandro woke to a wash of sunlight and a feeling of pure contentment.

Elena lay at his side, breathing gently. Alejandro gazed at her, unable to get enough of her. Even Coyotl was happy, lying sprawled at the bottom of Alejandro's mind, utterly spent and content.

Alejandro got out of bed. He dressed out of his suitcase, then wandered off to Elena's kitchen. The sea was sighing and washing against the shore, the water lightening under the summer dawn. Alejandro shuffled into the kitchen, trying to blink sleep out of his eyes and find the coffee maker.

Perambulating around the kitchen, his eyes fell on a display of photographs hung on the wall by the window. He paused, looking them over.

They seemed mainly family photographs. Elena as a young girl, posing with a woman he assumed was her mother, standing in a garden. Her mother standing by the shore, hair flying on the ocean breeze. A graduation picture, Elena holding her new degree. Smiling, Alejandro's eyes passed over each one—until they froze, hooked.

It showed Elena perhaps a few years younger than she was now. But she was not posing with a college degree, nor playing with a dog, nor even on dry land. This photograph showed her in the ocean. Sea water streamed off her tangled mane of hair, sparkled in some long-ago sunset that turned the ocean to peach and gold. The water perfectly complemented the rose-gold tail rising out of the surface, droplets raining down from the fanning, translucent fin.

"What are you doing?"

Alejandro jumped, then relaxed when he saw it was Elena, standing in the kitchen doorway and blinking sleepily. "Morning! I was just looking at your photos here." He pointed at the one depicting her as a mermaid. "I didn't know you were a mermaid!"

Her face went white. "What!"

"Hey, it's cool—I know lots of people are into that. There's mermaid tail couture these days, right? Do you still have a tail somewhere? Think I could see it?" He grinned, a wonderful thought occurring to him. "Actually, I'd love to see you *in* it! That would be awesome!" Coyotl, catching his enthusiasm, wriggled happily at the idea.

"Uh...right." Still looking a little shaky, Elena came further into the kitchen. "Yeah, I...used to be into that. Pretending to be a mermaid. But I—don't anymore."

"Really?" Alejandro was disappointed. "But you have so many paintings of you as a mermaid!"

"It's called imagination, Alejandro." Elena winked, her good humor restored. She looked at the photo, expression a little sad. "My mom took that photo of me. Before she passed."

"Oh, no. I'm sorry to hear that. What happened?"

"She drowned." Elena moved past him, starting to get the coffee together. "About two years ago."

"Drowned?" Alejandro blinked. "What happened?"

"She got caught underwater and stayed down too long."

"Was she into diving?"

"Oh, yeah. We've always spent a lot of time in the water in my family." Elena paused in coffee making to smile dreamily through the window at the sea. "I love the ocean," she murmured. "Maybe I should hate it after Mom, but...I love it. Mom always said the ocean gave birth to us, and it'll take us back when we die. It's just destiny. No point resenting it."

Alejandro looked at Elena, her face in shadow but still glowing, gazing out over the limitless ocean, every moment a brighter and brighter blue.

"That's beautiful," he said, with utmost sincerity.

The next few weeks were some of the happiest of Alejandro's life.

He kept his rental reservation, as it was too late to cancel without penalties, and he didn't want to impose on Elena. But he spent more time at Elena's house than at his rental, cooking, helping with cleaning, walking the shore and swimming, watching her paint and, of course, having the most amazing sex of his life.

Even Coyotl did not give trouble. It was some time until the dark of the moon, so the beast wasn't that strong. The combination of sex and Elena Seagraves kept Coyotl content and abased. The beast frisked and played in Alejandro's thoughts whenever Elena was around, his simple happiness amplifying Alejandro's more complex human emotions.

Everything about Elena Seagraves fascinated Alejandro and Coyotl both, from the sheen of sunlight in her hair, to the way she painted, peering at her canvas in utter concentration, deaf to the world around her, while entirely new worlds evolved to life under her brush. Alejandro could watch her for hours, or at least until she chased him away, laughing. The small house by the sea soon rang with their shared laughter, as habitual as the waves.

But of course they did not stay solely in the house. Elena took Alejandro around town, introducing him to her many friends, including other artists. Alejandro found a new vista opening before him: the world of artists and those who worked with them, their struggles and their triumphs. It was alien and fascinating to him, and he spent many happy hours observing this new species.

"Mark wants me to build a website for him," he said one night as he and Elena were walking home along the beach. They meandered with their shoes in their hands and their arms around each other, while darkness settled on the sea and the waxing moon rose above the bluff. "I think maybe I will."

"I thought you were in retirement." Elena nudged him. Coyotl yelped and leapt playfully at the contact—not that Elena was aware of that, of course.

Alejandro grinned sheepishly. "Maybe I'm not as ready to retire as I thought. Maybe I just need a career change."

"Good," said Elena with pleasure. "It's good to keep busy." She glanced at the dark ocean, the dim white waves. "Say, Alejandro…want to go swimming?"

"Right now?" laughed Alejandro, even as Coyotl leapt up at the chance to do anything with Elena. "It's so late! And we just went swimming earlier today."

"Along with about a hundred tourists. Come on, Alejandro, we'll have the sea to ourselves…" Elena was already dragging him down toward the water.

"We don't have swimsuits…"

"And so?" Elena's grin was bright as a star in the night. "It's dark."

Alejandro found himself grinning back. "So it is."

They left their clothes heaped on the beach and dived into the waves, the ocean lifting and caressing them, swimming along the glittering white path of the moon. Elena swam around Alejandro, swift as a fish, hair swirling behind her, and, just for a moment, he thought she truly was a mermaid.

About a week later, Elena came into the kitchen where Alejandro was cooking lunch, an unusually serious expression on her face.

"Alejandro," she said, "I've got to leave town today. I'll be gone overnight."

"Really?" Alejandro paused over the salad. Inside, Coyotl yelped with protest. "Where're you going, honey?"

"I have to meet with my agent." Elena gave a smile, but it lacked her usual warmth and conviction. "I'll be gone overnight, like I said. But I'll be back tomorrow."

"Seeing your agent requires an overnight stay?" Alejandro blinked.

"They live far away. But honestly, there's no need to worry! I'll be back tomorrow."

Alejandro wondered why she was so insistent on that point. "Well, okay, honey. I guess I'll see you tomorrow." He tried not to feel bereft. This was the first time she'd left him since they'd begun their affair. Coyotl whined in misery, pacing back and forth across Alejandro's mind.

"Thanks, Alejandro." Elena smiled again, a real smile this time, and came over to wrap her arms around his waist. "You're very sweet." She kissed him.

"Hey, work is work." He kissed her back, ignoring Coyotl's wretched crying. "And I should really spend some time in my actual rental, for a change."

They ate lunch together with good humor and then Alejandro saw Elena off in her car. He watched her back bumper disappear, loneliness and melancholy already settling over him. Only Coyotl to keep him company now— and the beast was sulking, his misery casting a pall over Alejandro's every thought.

Alejandro ate a lackluster meal in his cold, echoing rental. Perhaps he should have gone out, he reflected, looking around at the dusty surfaces he'd never bothered to place anything on. But the thought of going anywhere without Elena was miserable. He had to smile a little at this—what a difference a few weeks could make! Only a month ago, he hadn't thought anything of being alone or going out on his own. Now he felt like only half a person.

Coyotl wouldn't shut up, whining and crying and pacing around. Alejandro stood up. He had to do something to appease the beast, and exercise always helped. He headed outside.

The sun was setting in blazing glory, setting fire to the

sea. Alejandro wandered with a glass of wine, admiring the shimmering golds and reds. The sun blazed a radioactive yellow as it died, too brilliant to look at, and so he looked away, gazing inland until the spots before his eyes cleared away.

The moon had already risen, he realized. The full moon, which rose the moment the sun set. It glowed a cool white in the dark eastern sky.

The sun had drowned beneath the sea. Alejandro looked back, to the waves already turning dark blue under the indigo sky.

And so he saw the creature. Coyotl spotted it too, coming to sudden attention.

It was some enormous fish—no, a dolphin. But it wasn't swimming quite like a dolphin, not leaping out of the water in graceful arcs. It seemed to undulate sensually along the surface, its great, fanlike tail rising from the water, its hair trailing along—

Its *hair*?

Alejandro screwed his eyes shut, so hard that red spots bloomed before his vision. *It's not real,* he told himself. *I did not just see a mermaid swim by.*

But Coyotl's curiosity forced his eyes open again. The ocean was empty, the waves blank of any creatures, supernatural or otherwise.

Alejandro breathed a deep sigh of relief. He must have been imagining things. He supposed he *had* been spending a lot of time around Elena's mermaid art…

Still, perhaps it was time to head inside. Ignoring Coyotl's urges to go down and investigate, Alejandro turned and marched back to his rental, resolutely not looking at the sea.

The next day, Alejandro hurried to Elena's house, Coyotl nearly insane with eagerness. To their shared delight, her car was in the driveway.

Alejandro nearly ran to the door, pushed it half open. "Elena! Elena…"

"I'm here," came her voice from the living room, and Alejandro rushed in.

"You're back!" He leaned down to kiss her, sitting on the sofa. "How was your trip?"

Elena smiled wanly. She seemed tired, leaning back on the sofa, face drawn. "Honestly? Exhausting."

"It was just an overnight trip, right?"

"You don't know my agent," said Elena with a wry twist to her lips.

She shifted, and her scent rose, reaching Alejandro's nose. He sniffed, and Coyotl sniffed deeper still. There was something decidedly…different about Elena's scent today. She often smelled of the sea, but today the salt-scent was deeper, accompanied by the scent of fish scales…Had she been eating at a seafood restaurant? But this didn't smell precisely the same.

A wild idea occurred to Alejandro, a mad, lunatic idea.

Could she be...? Could she possibly be...? He pushed the thought down, making Coyotl growl with frustration. The beast wanted to investigate further.

"Well, you're back now." Alejandro flopped down on the sofa beside Elena. She lounged against him, arms going around his neck. "What do you want to do now?" he asked, hoping he already knew the answer.

"Screw you senseless," she murmured in his ear.

After that, neither Alejandro nor Coyotl cared what she smelled like.

It was only much later, when they'd fallen off the sofa and the sun was advancing across the floor in golden squares and Elena was dozing in his arms, that Alejandro remembered that he too would need to be out of town overnight. In two weeks.

"I'll be out of town overnight," Alejandro said to Elena two weeks later.

Elena looked up from her canvas, sea-colored eyes surprised. "Really? What for?"

"I've got to go see a family member." Alejandro fought not to wriggle and writhe all over Elena's studio. As the moon had waned, Coyotl had grown stronger, more restless, scratching against Alejandro's mind, worrying at the barrier between them as it grew more tenuous. "It'll only take a night."

Elena was still staring at him. Alejandro's—or, rather, Coyotl's—senses had grown sharper as the moon waned, and he could very nearly smell her surprise and disappointment. "Maybe I could come with you?"

"Not to see this family member," said Alejandro, honestly enough. "Trust me, I'm the only one they can handle."

Elena gave an unwilling snort of laughter. "Like that, huh?" She tucked her paintbrush behind her ear and rose to wrap her arms around him. "I'll miss you."

"I'll miss you too." Alejandro embraced her, not entirely of his own volition. Coyotl panted with lust and urgency inside him, urging him to throw Elena down, tear her clothes off and fuck her senseless—

Alejandro tensed, muscles going rigid. With a massive effort, he let go of Elena and stepped away. Coyotl screamed with frustration and Elena looked slightly startled. "I'll see you tomorrow, okay, sweetie?" Alejandro forced a smile.

"Of course." Elena's own smile looked somewhat forced as well. "I'll see you then."

Late that afternoon, Alejandro drove away from the coast, heading to an inland state park. He'd scouted this place out before coming to Santa Rosales, and knew it was perfect, with acres of empty chaparral, hills and canyons, and very few park rangers.

He parked outside of the actual park, where he would not be ticketed or towed, and headed into the park's confines. He took no supplies with him, no equipment. He bounded up the dirt paths, Coyotl bouncing with energy inside him, while the afternoon waned into a long, warm twilight.

Alejandro found an outcrop of large, dusty boulders, overlooking a gully. The scent of fresh water hit his nostrils, and he let out an involuntary yip, body shivering with excitement. He hushed Coyotl down. *Not yet. Soon.*

Coyotl subsided with a sulky snap of his nonexistent jaws. Alejandro climbed under the outcrop, and, in a shallow cave, stripped off, folding his clothes and piling them neatly out of sight. Hiding away his clothes—and remembering where he'd hidden them—was important.

Naked, Alejandro crouched in the cave and waited. Around him, the shadows lengthened and deepened. The scents of the park—dust, shrubs, stone, heat and water— washed over his nostrils, making him twitch. The sound of nearby traffic rushed in his ears. Lights bloomed miles away, in nearby towns and neighborhoods, and overhead the first stars began peeking out.

But only when the sun finally sank beneath the horizon did Coyotl emerge.

Alejandro let out a cry that was half yowl, half human scream, as the transformation seized hold, ripping through him, overwhelming him like a Pacific wave.

Night had fallen completely. Lights glowed in the towns and along the highway, but in the park, darkness reigned, without even the moon to lighten it.

A small, slim shape darted out from the outcrop. It paused, testing the air in its fur, sniffing the wind. Then, scenting prey, it let out an excited yelp and ran down into the gully on all fours.

Alejandro awoke with the taste of rabbit blood in his mouth. He was half-dangling off a boulder over the stream, his hair trailing in the water below. He was scratched up, the energy flow of the night before still washing through him.

Yeah, pretty typical of the morning after.

Moaning, he struggled up, his wet hair sticking to his back. Inside, Coyotl had gone to sleep, curled up in contentment after his night of fun and games. Alejandro was almost sad. Coyotl was a nuisance, but Alejandro always missed him when he went to sleep during the days after the dark of the moon. It was strange, being alone inside his own head.

Alejandro washed in the stream, splashing cold water over himself and getting off the worst of the dust, dead leaves and broken twigs. Then he began hiking back up the hill, to the outcrop and his clothes.

Alejandro dressed and made his way back to his car, getting used to being in human form again as he walked. He drove straight back to Santa Rosales. Coyotl had hunted and eaten well last night, so he wasn't hungry. But he was desperate to see Elena again.

As he pulled up before Elena's house, though, he felt a flash of anxiety. Suppose Elena didn't want to see him? Suppose she was angry? Suppose she'd dumped him for some hot young surfer with abs like steel, who graced the covers of magazines and modeled for ocean conservation campaigns?

But all his fears were unfounded. Elena came running out even as he was climbing out of his car, catching him up in a hug. "Alejandro! I missed you!"

"I missed you too, sweetie!" Alejandro returned her hug fully and gave her a kiss. "Oh, it's good to see you."

Elena gave a self-conscious giggle. "Wow, we're like an old couple, aren't we? Can't stay away from each other for a single night!"

"Ah, there's worse things to be than an old couple." Alejandro slammed the car door behind him and started to walk Elena inside, one arm around her shoulders.

"Where's your luggage?" Elena craned back. "And how's that relative of yours doing?"

For a moment, Alejandro's mind went blank. Then he remembered his cover story. "Oh. They're fine. Just…cranky. And I dropped my stuff off at my rental." For a moment he was pinched with guilt for lying to Elena like this, but there was no way he could tell her the truth.

To distract her, he hugged her again, sniffing her hair.

"Mm, you've been swimming this morning, haven't you?" He could smell the salt.

"You have such a good sense of smell!" She grinned up at him.

Alejandro felt another pinch of guilt. "Yeah, I guess I do."

They went inside, while the sun rose over the coyote-haunted hills and cast long rays over the wild sea.

"I'll be out of town again," Elena said two weeks later.

Alejandro looked up from his laptop, eyes bleary from concentration. He was getting his new business set up, and it consumed most of his waking hours. Add that to making plans to sell his old condo and move in with Elena, and it was no wonder he'd lost track of time somewhat.

"Got to see your agent again?" He pushed Coyotl down, whining and scratching with curiosity. Coyotl had awoken after his dark-moon nap and, with the upcoming full moon, was restless and energetic once more.

"That's right." Elena was avoiding his gaze. She began moving around the kitchen, getting lunch together. "Alejandro…"

"Yeah, sweetie?" Alejandro looked up again.

"If I…If I told you I had a…condition…"

"What kind of condition?" Alejandro sat up in sudden alarm. "Elena…is it…you're not…?"

"Oh, no!" She grinned in reassurance. "No, nothing like

that. I'm perfectly healthy. It's just…well…"

"You don't have to tell me," Alejandro said when the silence stretched too long. He felt a surge of hurt that he quelled. It wasn't like he wasn't keeping secrets from Elena, after all. "But Elena, I am okay with any conditions you might have. I love you, and nothing's going to change that."

"Thanks, Alejandro." She smiled quickly. "You're such a wonderful person."

"Not as wonderful as you." He abandoned his laptop to wrap her in a hug. Her scent washed over him: shampoo and Elena-scent, but overlaid with something strange. Fish scales. And the sea.

Just like last month.

That night, lying in Elena's bed, Alejandro couldn't sleep.

Coyotl was partly to blame of course, rattling around his subconscious, growling at the full moon. But Elena's words kept echoing in his mind. What "condition" did she have that she couldn't share with Alejandro? What had been that scent, wafting off her? And why did she have to leave town once again, on this night of the month?

Could it be…? Could it possibly be…?

Alejandro crushed the hope ruthlessly. Ever since his grandfather had died, leaving him and Coyotl alone in the world, he'd cherished irrational hopes of meeting others like him. But they all came to naught. Abuelo had been the only other one like him, and to hope for others was to be constantly lonely and disappointed.

But still…maybe?

He couldn't sleep. The bed felt too hot, Coyotl too restless. He sat up, pulled on his clothes and stumbled out.

Outside, the moon flooded the night, sparkling on the waves. Alejandro walked down toward the beach, driven by Coyotl's energy. A rabbit darted out across his path, and he made an involuntary lunge, startling it away. Coyotl whined.

Down at the beach, there came a splash.

Alejandro froze, Coyotl coming to attention inside him. Then, both their curiosities roused, Alejandro and Coyotl ran down to the shore.

The tide was high, washing over the beach. Alejandro paused, listening and sniffing. There was something in the water, he was sure of it, something large and near the shore.

Then he saw it, passing across the path of moonlight. A huge tailed something, gliding across the white glitter.

Alejandro ran down to the water's edge. He couldn't stop himself. Coyotl was just too curious, all his hunter's instincts roused. The man and the beast inside him ran into the water, cold waves splashing up around them, to lunge down and grab the huge fish-thing.

In his hands, Elena stared up at Alejandro with vast, shocked blue-green eyes. Her hair flowed around her, jeweled with foam, trailing in the water. Behind her, her muscular tail beat the waves with a fanlike fin.

For a moment they were frozen, the man and the

mermaid, the ocean washing around them. Then Elena cleared her throat.

"Hi, Alejandro. This, um, isn't what it looks like." She paused, reconsidering. "Well, okay. It's exactly what it looks like."

Later, Alejandro sat cross-legged on a barnacle-encrusted boulder. Below him, Elena clung on, her tail still submerged.

"So…you're a mermaid shifter?" Alejandro asked.

"Yep. Like all the women in my family. I turn into a mermaid at the full moon. I can transform at other times too, but at the full moon it's obligatory."

Alejandro couldn't take his eyes off her tail, glittering and shining in the moonlight. Inside, Coyotl sniffed curiously. "It's—it's real? Your tail?"

"Yeah. Feel it if you want." Elena moved into position. When Alejandro hesitated, she let out an exasperated sigh. "Come on, Alejandro, it's not like you've never felt up my ass before."

Alejandro let out a startled laugh at this, and got the courage to reach down and touch her tail. It was real. No synthetic mermaid tail could possibly replicate such cold, slimy scales, the impossible muscles bunching and pulling underneath, the structure of bones that were most definitely not human legs. Alejandro felt it up and down, marveling, Coyotl dancing with interest and curiosity. "Wow. This is amazing."

The mermaid regarded him. "You're being awfully calm about this."

"Really? I kind of thought I was freaking out."

"No, Alejandro. Freaking out would be running for the hills, shrieking about monsters." Bitterness edged Elena's voice. "That's what my dad did. And my grandfather."

"Really?" Alejandro scowled in disapproval, and Coyotl let out an indignant yelp. "That's ridiculous! What's wrong with turning into a mermaid once a month? It's not like you're turning into a dangerous predator, not like me—" He broke off.

"Alejandro?" said Elena when he'd been quiet too long.

Alejandro withdrew his hand, curling up around himself. Inside, Coyotl cowered with fear and dread. He couldn't look at Elena. He took a deep breath, ignoring Coyotl's urgent, pleading yelps. He could hardly believe he was about to say this.

"You're not the only shifter in the world," he said. "The men in my family...we're shifters too. We turn into coyotes at the dark of the moon."

There was a long silence, broken only by the swish of the sea. Alejandro didn't dare look at Elena. Coyotl let out a long, silent howl.

"Really?" Elena's laugh startled him into glancing at her again. She was grinning in the water, eyes shining. "So *that's* where you were two weeks ago? Running around as a coyote all night?"

"Y–yeah." Alejandro managed to nod. "In a state park."

"Wow!" Elena laughed again and, after a moment, Alejandro joined her, their voices rising above the waves. Coyotl danced with relief and happiness, yipping.

"You know, you're the first person I've ever told," Alejandro said when they'd calmed. "Aside from my Abuelo, that is. He raised me, and taught me all the tricks to control my condition."

"Mom did the same for me," Elena said. "And you're the first person *I've* ever told. Or, rather, the first person who ever found out." She gave him a filthy look.

"Look, I'm sorry, okay? Coyotl doesn't come out at the full moon, but he gets restless. I had to take a walk to calm him down, and then we heard the splashing."

"Wait." Elena blinked. "Is your...Do you think the coyote is separate from you somehow?"

"He *is*," said Alejandro. "He spends most of his time in my subconscious, awake or asleep at different times of the month. Sometimes he's more restless than others." He cocked his head. "But for you—the mermaid isn't separate from your human self?"

"Not at all! Wow, we've both got a lot to learn, don't we?"

"So..." Alejandro wet his lips. Coyotl whined with hope. "So you...you want to stay together? Even now?"

"Well, of course," said Elena, like there had never been any question. "A mermaid and a were-coyote? We're perfect for each other!"

Alejandro couldn't stop the grin unfurling across his face.

Coyotl sang for joy. "Well, *perfect* might be me turning into a merman, not a coyote."

"Let's not ask for too much." They laughed together, under the full moon. "Seriously, though, you might be the one man I can actually make a life with. Any ordinary human guy would run screaming. Or pretend to be okay with it before turning me in for experiments."

"And any ordinary human woman would do the same to me," said Alejandro, thinking of his own long-vanished mother. He reached down, touching the mermaid's cold, salt-wet hand. "Elena…I love you. Coyotl loves you. We both want to stay with you for the rest of our lives."

Elena reached over with her other hand, taking his wrist. "And I want to do the same. My lovely coyote-man."

"My lovely mermaid." Alejandro leaned over to kiss the top of her head. Coyotl howled with approval.

They hovered linked together at the edge of land and sea, beneath the full moon, while the mermaid's tail beat the water and the coyote danced and sang within.

Blueberry Bells
EF DEAL

The path through the scrub pines down to the beach wound and twisted exactly as Benjamin remembered. After so many years, he was surprised to find it unchanged. Lowbush blueberry blossoms quivered in the onshore breeze, silent white bells tolling his passing. Benjamin savored the rich scents of the Barrens—cedar, hemlock, pitch pine, the sugar sand—the years falling away from him, carrying him back to a time when it was all fresh and new, and he thought it would never end. Or at least, that it would have ended differently.

He was seventeen, rich, spoiled, angry at the world, and railing against the forces of destiny that had dragged him from the elite of Cambridge to slave away in a steam engine factory in New Jersey, putting his education to "meaningful purpose," as his father phrased it. The factory prospered, and he was swiftly promoted to a position of some esteem, but

amid the metal, the melted brass, the constant barrage of pistons, Benjamin stubbornly clutched his raging fury to his breast. He made himself unwelcome at every tavern along the shore routes, and while his work did not reflect his bitterness, he found himself friendless and cold. He had had every intention of slipping away to New York City, from there to find a means of sailing to London. Had he let it slip in a fit of anger? Someone had warned his father, who cut off his allowance, forcing him to live on his salary alone, the habit of which had left him wanting.

When spring came the following year, he decided to walk into the ocean and drown himself, but having no notion of how far a journey that was on foot, he decided to settle for angrily striding along the brackish Manasquan beach.

Benjamin was no longer angry. The years had stripped him of pride, rage, hunger, ambition...of everything but one memory that guided his steps along the sandy trail. The Barrens were alive with the calls of whippoorwills, warblers and wood thrush. Eagles and hawks cried overhead. The raucous noise of gulls soon drowned them out as he emerged from the woods into the marshy sands of the river's edge. He halted to take in the new yet familiar scape of tall grasses, rushes, cattails, a massive flock of snow geese gibbering on the water, a pair of osprey on the wing. Summer peeked up over the horizon, nudging spring into the past.

He found the ancient log where they used to sit, night after night, so he lit a small fire and waited. As the sun slid below the trees behind him, indigo dusk covered the bog-iron-stained water. A slice of moon appeared in the evening blue sky.

"Now," Benjamin thought, "now, she'll come. She has to."

The flames leached the last of his anger. Spring frogs filled the quiet with a chorus of peeping. Small splashes betrayed furtive turtles, terrapins, and bass. For the first time in a long time, Benjamin knew serenity, felt he was part of the world around him. In that moment, her tender hand touched his shoulder.

"Are you all right?"

He looked up into the face of a woman perhaps three times his age dressed in a light summer gown, her white hair undone and falling to her waist, lifted by the breeze. The firelight gave her a golden glow.

She smiled then, a calming smile. Relieved, not amused. Reassuring, not mocking. "I see I've startled you. May I sit?"

He gained his feet and indicated his own seat, but instead she sat on the sand across from him. Sand covered the wet hem of her day gown as well as her bare feet like sugar on pastries.

"Benjamin Willis," he introduced himself, and he bowed.

"Yes, Benjamin," she said with mild surprise. "How have you been since last we met?"

They had never met, of course. He had thought the poor woman had lost her mind, wandering in an illusory haze of memories. He had humored her through the next hour as she spoke to him of snow geese, of spring peepers, of the clever gulls who plucked mussels from the briny edge and flew them into the air, only to drop them on the worn path to crack them open. Clever gulls. She told him of the terrapins' journey into the sands, and he pictured the hatchlings racing to the waters before the clever gulls could take them. And when she spoke of blueberry blossoms ringing their silent antiphon, he heard their gentle tintinnabulation like the tinkling of fairies' wings. By evening's end he'd wondered if he was the one who had lost time and memory somehow. He'd remembered blueberries he had never seen, grown fat with summer's sun and the sweet soil of the sugar sand.

Of course they had met. Of course he remembered her.

"Emmaline."

"There, you see?" she said. "We are old friends, you and I."

They were old friends. Had they ever kissed? Were they lovers? Surely Benjamin would have remembered her. Not like the girls in the taverns. Not like his aging landlady. Emmaline—warm, tender, serene and somehow timeless, like the forest, like the ocean, like the cycle of springs, returning to this moment, this place.

"You've been waiting for your husband," he recalled. "You haven't found him yet?"

Every night, from spring through autumn, Emmaline strolled the sands, her eyes sweeping the horizon for ships, combing the sands for signs, searching the edge of the Barrens as if waiting for him to descend the winding, twisted path.

She gazed out over the eastern horizon. "I have not."

"Perhaps his ship was lost."

She didn't answer right away as she swept north to south. Then she turned to him with her calm smile. "No, Benjamin. It's not his ship that is lost. I'll find him."

A song rose from the river's edge, carried on the breeze. Benjamin stood to watch her graceful steps as she danced with the soft lapping waves, singing the songs the blueberry bells had taught them. The years had not touched her. He looked down at his own worn hands. More than years had taken him.

"My father," he told her, his voice edged with an anger he would not let her see because she was softness and light, and he would not bruise her, "has chosen a bride for me. In Boston."

"Yes, Benjamin. You told me."

"But I've only just—"

He stopped. Had he told her? Did she already know? Perhaps he had done; perhaps he would do again. She confounded him with her serene smile and clear blue eyes. Blueberry eyes. Time had passed, spring turned to summer, and summer to autumn as golden as her silvery hair by firelight. How many summers? How many fires? How many hatchlings or blueberries?

Benjamin married Sarah Dudley. He was twenty-three. She was seventeen, rich, spoiled, angry at the world and railing against the forces of destiny that had forced her into marriage to a man she did not love. She had planned to slip away to Long Wharf, there to find the means to sail to Europe. Instead she bore a son, or tried to. Both of them slipped away in death before the first wedding anniversary.

Why had he waited so long to return? Why had he not turned his back on the Dudley fortune and taken back the serenity of Emmaline's smile? What could he say to her? Family obligations, financial security, a legacy, an established reputation…Would Emmaline care for any of those reasons, when the blueberry bells chimed like fairies' wings?

And here again was Emmaline, still searching for her husband by the shores. Benjamin did not know how to greet her, how to explain himself, how to renew the golden aura of the firelight as she came closer, her hair flowing in the breeze, her face smooth and soft, her smile calm and reassuring.

"Are you all right?" she asked, searing closed the abyss of years that had separated them.

He couldn't find words to tell her. No. It had all gone wrong, a life quietly spent in desperate loneliness, smothered in a cold city that held no music for him, and a death of desperate tragedy, isolated in the family mansion, buffered by wealth and good fortune, buffeted by an emptiness he could not name until he found himself on the familiar winding, twisting path that cut through the Barrens to lead him to the forever summer, to life, to her.

Benjamin answered, "I am now." He bowed, as if in apology. "I've been lost too. I don't have anything to offer you, no substance. I have nothing." He shook off his self-recriminations. "But, you, have you found him, Emmaline?"

She reached up to caress his face. He searched her blueberry eyes for recognition. She kissed him. He melted into the warmth of her lips that tasted of tangy salt and sugar. Tenderly, he held her as the moon peeked up over the horizon, casting ghost dancers on the waters around them. When they parted, she laid her head on his breast.

"Oh, yes. I've finally found him."

He stroked her hair. "I'm so sorry. I didn't realize until now. I could only hope…"

"Shh."

She took his hand and led him from the shore, up the path through scrub pines into the Barrens, where the chimes of ghostly blueberry bells sang them into eternity together.

Author Bios

Jenna Andrews found the sunny Gulf coast of Naples in April of 2006. Since then, she has divided her time between Florida and the sugary white beaches of New Jersey. She enjoys playing tennis, reading at the beach, bike rides to the Point with her husband and a nice glass of wine at sunset.

Maureen Bowden is a Liverpudlian, living with her musician husband in North Wales. She has had 182 stories and poems accepted by paying markets and she was nominated for the 2015 *International Pushcart Prize*. In 2019, *Hiraeth Books* published an anthology of her stories, *Whispers of Magic*, and they will be publishing an anthology of her poems in the near future. She also writes song lyrics, mostly comic political satire, set to traditional melodies. Her husband has performed them in folk music clubs throughout the UK. She loves her family and friends, rock 'n' roll, Shakespeare, and cats.

Leigh Calvin has loved to read since the 5th grade when she first read *Are You There God, It's Me Margaret* by Judy Blume. She first tried her hand at writing for fun a few years ago when she created her blog, *Donkeys To College*. She had tens of followers and was well known among people who already knew her. Her biggest fan and biggest heckler was her mother. Leigh is married to this cute guy she met at college. They have two grown children who are not criminals (as far as she knows), so she feels pretty pleased with her parenting. It's a low bar. Besides reading and writing, Leigh loves to play tennis, travel and spend time in Long Beach Island, NJ.

Adrienne Clarke: A past winner of the Alice Munro short fiction contest, Adrienne's work has appeared in several publications including, *New Plains Review*, *Silly Tree Anthologies*, and in the e-zines *The Devilfish Review*, *Rose Red Review*, *Carmina Magazine*, and *The Long Island Literary Journal*. Her first YA novel, *Losing Adam*, garnered a silver medal in the 2018 *Independent Publisher Book Awards* and was selected as a finalist in the *Eric Hoffer Book Awards*.

Ef Deal's short fiction has been published in numerous online zines and anthologies as well as in *F&SF*. Her short story "Czesko" was given honorable mention in Gardner Dozois' *Year's Best Science Fiction and Fantasy*. Ef has been freelance line-editing and copy-editing for over thirty years. She is currently assistant fiction editor at *Abyss & Apex* magazine, and video editor for *Strong Women ~ Strange Worlds*. Her first novel *Esprit de Corpse* is available from *eSpec Books*, the first in a French steampunk paranormal romance series involving the Twins of Bellefées. When she's not writing, Ef marches old-school alumni drum and bugle corps on soprano bugle; she also composes, arranges and directs music. She lives in Haddonfield, NJ, with her husband and two chows. She is an associate member of SFWA and an affiliate member of HWA.

Natalie Zellat Dyen began writing humor pieces and essays for newspapers while working as a technical writer. Since turning to fiction, her work has appeared in a number of publications including, *Philadelphia Stories*, *The MacGuffin*, the *Schuylkill Valley Journal*, *Willow Review*, *Alternative Truths: Endgame, Jewish Writing Project, Damselfly, CERASUS Magazine, Every Day Fiction*, and *Neshaminy : The Bucks County Historical and Literary Journal.* Her short story collection, *Finding Her Voice*, was published in 2019. Her historical fiction novel, *Locked in Silence*, will be released in February 2024.

Jocelyne Gregory lives on the Sunshine Coast of British Columbia and writes speculative fiction and poetry. As a child, she'd search libraries for stories she wanted to read and when she couldn't find them, she'd write them herself. She holds an MFA in Creative Writing from UBC's School of Creative Writing, and a writing certificate from Simon Fraser University's *The Writer's Studio*. She works as a manuscript consultant with *The Writer's Studio* and community libraries. She's written reviews for *Young Adulting*. Her work has appeared in *50-Word Stories, Emerge16, New Zealand's Flash Fiction, The Dancing Plague: A Collection of Utter Speculation, Zooscape,* and *BraveNewGirls* (2023). Two of her short science fiction stories received honourable mentions for the *L. R. Hubbard Writer's of the Future Contest* in the 3rd and 4th quarters of 2022. A trailer she made won Best Trailer at the *Swedish International Film Festival* in 2023.

Valerie Hunter teaches high school English and has had stories and poems in publications including *Room*, *Beneath Ceaseless Skies*, and *Sonder*, as well as multiple anthologies.

Melanie Mulrooney lives in Nova Scotia with her husband and a gaggle of kids. When not herding children or writing stories, she can be found with her nose in a book, researching her latest special interest, or begging her family to play a board game. She loves the smell of wood smoke, that first sip of tea in the morning, and the sound of laughing babies.

Simon Quinn is a proud graduate of Northern Arizona University. He delighted in studying subjects that could help him tell better puns: English, Creative Writing, and Geology. As a disabled, queer writer, he focuses on representing people like him in his works. In his free time, he enjoys making his own tea blends, playing with his extremely fluffy cat, painting various sharks, and collecting heart shaped rocks.

Janice Rider (she/her) has always loved the natural world and resides in Calgary, Alberta, Canada, close to the Rocky Mountains. She has a BSc in Zoology with a minor in English

Literature and a BEd degree with a science teaching specialty. Janice directs The Chameleon Drama Club for children and youth. Three of her plays for youth have been published through *Eldridge Plays and Musicals*. As well, a nonfiction piece of hers on snakes was published in *Honeyguide Literary Magazine*. Two of Janice's short stories have been published. One story about a giant millipede was released in the anthology, *Beware the Bugs*, through *Word Balloon Books*. The other story is in the *North American Jules Verne Society's* anthology, *Extraordinary Visions*.

Rose Strickman is a speculative fiction author living in Seattle, Washington. Her work has appeared in anthologies such as *Sword and Sorceress 32*, *Gilded Glass*, *The Devil You Know Better* and *Still of Winter*. She has also been published in several e-zines, and self-published several novellas.

When she isn't playing around in fictional worlds, **C.N. Wheaton** can often be found teaching science to recalcitrant teens or doing beach clean-ups. She also sporadically blogs about storytelling on her blog. Her writing has appeared in *The Fantastic Other*, *Humour Me*, and *Daily Science Fiction*.

Check out the Collections of Utter Speculation

The Lost Colony of Roanoke

The Jersey Devil

Lady in White

The Dancing Plague

And our other Books

Incubate: a horror collection of feminine power

Work in Progress: Story Crafting Notebook

www.speculationpub.com